Unimagined tales... some from twisted minds

PJ Ramírez

All rights reserved. The total or partial reproduction of this work is not allowed, nor its incorporation into a computer system, or its transmission in any form or by any means (electronic, mechanical, photocopying, recording, or otherwise) without the prior written permission of the copyright holder is a violation of these rights and may constitute a crime against intellectual property

The content of this work is the responsibility of the author and does not necessarily reflect the views of the publishing house. All texts and images were provided by the author, who is solely responsible for their rights.

Published by Ibukku, LLC
www.ibukku.com
Graphic Design: Diana Patricia González J.
Cover Design: Ángel Flores Guerra B.
Copyright © 2023 PJ Ramírez
ISBN Paperback: 978-1-68574-442-7
ISBN Hardcover: 978-1-68574-444-1
ISBN eBook: 978-1-68574-443-4

Table of Contents

Disclaimer	5
The Strange Attempt	7
The Young Witch	31
Salmonella	45
Tammuz	61
Yuri	81
Sadiel	85
Ivanno	95
The whoremother	107
High School Poet	113
Wrong Incision	119
The Colombian Girl	139
The Knot	153
Gay Obsession	175

Disclaimer

The characters in the stories that follow have been produced for the fiction purposes only. Any relation to reality is coincidental. The product presented in this collection of tales have been produced and edited by an indie writer, me. Efforts have been made to get the best entertaining results, with study, practice, and analysis. The syntaxes could have some flaws for which I will thank the readers if they drop me a short notice to agentindie2018@gmail.com.

This set of stories have been copyrighted for the proper entitlement and authorship property.

The Strange Attempt
By Pedro J. Ramírez

The whole staff was meeting, each of them very reputed. Some of them were famous as healers of almost any illness known these days. Doctor Soff was a non-traditional physician. He felt free, without minding the criticisms of others, to look into nature's way of healing, traditional medicines, and supernatural causes. He also stood aside because he had been greatly commended in his military roles. With the case at hand, he understood that it was supernatural and would have to invoke his attributes as a medium of spirits. No cause was found, yet the woman has been swelling for three days. In a few more days, her skin tissue will rip and her organs will bleed and some could be spit out of her. She was a woman of good looks as shown in her license pictures. In person, her body was that of an attractive woman, by shape and proportions. He was framed within the walls of a typical hospital, with the health professionals in white going and coming, beds on the sides with moaning patients, syringes, and pots of medicines. But this environment did not make him a man for conventional medicine.

Weeks ago, the doctor approached the woman while in bed and he could feel her spiritual disturbances. The causes of her illness were from spirits, regardless of what the other physicians said or speculated. The doctor frequently talked to the woman.

"My dear, what are you feeling?" he asked her days ago.

"I don't know, really," she answered more freely as she familiarized herself with him, "My symptoms are erratic. I may feel headaches, and pain in my back, one or both legs may get paralyzed, and sometimes I have been blinded for a few minutes... despair. I don't know what to expect. The swelling is in the worst state. It is constant and without pain."

With equal freedom, he diagnosed, privately, "Dear, your condition is not from nature. Nothing in your body produces your condition. All instruments and analyses have been done on blood, urine, and saliva. From these, nothing indicated that you have a body problem. I have to comment to you though, that when I get close to you, I feel that your spirit had been affected by other spirits. This seems to come from a curse from somebody who wants to destroy you. That is, either kill you or ruin your spiritual or emotional life or both. But they are having a hard time with that. You have a spiritual shield. I figure that they will try something physical against you, trying to make you vulnerable. That will be soon."

"Why would somebody want to hurt me? I don't offend or aggravate people's life. At least not by design," she said with humble signs.

"Hahaha, 'not by design.' Are you an engineer? Those are engineering terms. Let me rephrase. Is there anybody interested in something that you have or competing against you for something that you could call 'good' or 'for good profits'?" She was amused by his engineering comment, smiling briefly.

"Actually I am a student of engineering. And YES. There is something of great benefit and there is something that I will call *good*. For-profit, there is an invention that can process ten thousand times what an optic fiber processes now." It was inevitable for her to express herself in engineering economic terms. "That represents substantial savings in cabling, operators, and a long chain of related services. At the other extreme, for good, there is a man with whom I am involved. We had experienced intimacies and I got pregnant. I delivered a boy. The baby is in England under the care of my aunt to keep him away from these spiritual influences. The relationship was short-lived. It was mostly physical. But somebody envied that and wants to have that man exclusively. That woman has confronted me expressing her interest in him. She has threatened me with the supernatural like I am now. She wants me to die. Meanwhile, she lures him with her good looks, which are better than mine."

"Jesus. You are so attractive yet you consider yourself less than her. Why is it that every woman considers she is less than others? Each person has the treats that correspond and generally, they match well. You are attractive. Very. I am glad to be here with you. Do not you remember me?"

"I do remember you, definitely. I sense that luring waves come from you to me. Am I right? My name is Mariely."

"I know your name, Mariely. I remember you from my younger years. Not that I feel old but some time has passed since I knew you in high school. You are very sensitive to spiritual matters. I also feel that you do not disapprove of my waves. Am I right?" asked Doctor Soff.

"You are right. But in my case, I have learned about love and the implications and complications of it," staring at him, "but you have not. You have been avoiding it. That could make you suffer. You have never experienced loving." Her assertions did not make sense to him but they showed her as more mature and experienced than doctor Soff.

"Aside from all this, there is a lot of work that we have to do. Those spirits surrounding you need to be exiled to their realms. Their role is to get you sick and make you die. You need to live for your baby."

"Agreed. I believe that this wave of spirits is to annihilate me to get my child." Mariely replied.

"Let's start, then. Tell me all you can about your past. No matter how unimportant a detail may be for you," said Doctor Soff. She felt free talking with the doctor. His attractiveness and soft speaking have broken all walls created by time.

Mariely started her story. Mostly biographical. She grew up in the same old neighborhood that he had. Most of the residents were families of oldies. Parents were around sixty-five or seventy years. All were related. For the same reason, their relations were affected by the internal feuds of the families. In her case, the feud was because of love affairs. Mariely fell in love with a very attractive man who decided to join the military and left without giving word to her. Another man, Gerard, started rapping her and she decided to turn to him letting him take the place of the military. He was a handsome and well-built man with a very keen intelligence. He had the additional blessing of belonging to a well-to-do family. She still remembered the military man but the immediate advantages of Gerard prompted her to have a relationship with him. She was not shy to admit that she had been in bed with Gerard, got pregnant with the first intercourse, and had a male baby.

"I had a beautiful boy. Him and I had many ideas for the future of the child. But there was a woman, Karina, who had been after the affection of Gerard. He was not interested in her but she was determined to lay him and get pregnant. She really wanted to trap him. It was not a matter of love. It was a contest for the trophy that he was among the young women of those days."

"You mean that if you had not mentioned what happened with Gerard, this lady, Karina, would not be after him," said Doctor Soff.

"It happened because I was so presumptuous that attracted his attention. She took an opportunity at a party in her home, led him to a secret room of her father, and seduced him. When she had him with a powerful erection, she jumped on him and raped him. Then came back to the main room to tell the story of her experience. But she did not get pregnant. Now she wants to claim a victory by hurting my health and getting me dead. She is a spoiled girl. She is using high-level spiritual forces."

"What does Gerard say of all this? What about you and him," asked Soff. Soff noticed that she already was more open in her communications. He felt waves of heat in him every time that he pleased himself scanning her body. Her figure was very appealing.

"Nothing. He got into sexual vices tearing as many hymens as available. He gave up on me. He just wants to eat pussies and once in a while ram the ass of those who want to stay virgins. They are waiting in line for him," answered Mariely. "But Karina is persistent and wants to have the man, regardless. She wants him to get her pregnant. I fear for my baby. This woman has some evil relatives in the spiritual and natural realms and these could hurt anybody on her whim. They do not abide by the law and her family is very powerful. Now Gerard does not seem concerned about the baby." While she was telling her colorful story, a man of square jaw walked in; a police officer.

"Is a person in here, I reckon has to be a woman, whose name is Mariely?"

She responded spontaneously. "I am. What are you looking me for?" she asked. The officer was startled when he saw her.

Now composed, the officer asked, "Do you have a son, a baby son, in England?"

"Yes." Wrinkles now showed on her forehead. "Why your question?"

"We have been informed that your baby had been abducted. Interpol is investigating now. They got information that the baby is yours. The person who was taking care of the baby had been grossly assassinated. The criminal cut the throat of the person caring for the baby. Do you have an idea of who could be the perpetrator?"

"No. I have an idea of people who would be interested in having my baby," tears started to roll down her cheeks. "But they are locals and I have not learned that they had gone to England. That is why the baby is living there with my aunt. I am waiting to get over my illness to join them."

The officer took notice of her tears. "The person assassinated was not female. It was a man of the Negro race. Was your aunt supposed to be with the baby?" the officer asked. "There are no traces of a woman related to the abduction."

"If my aunt was not there, how did you come to know that I am the mother?" asked Mariely.

"Somebody left a note with printed letters from different magazines telling about you and where to locate you. Here are the photos from Interpol." Opening an envelope to display the evidence. "You can see the pictures here and the cadaver of the Negro. His name is Ottuga, African. It seems that he was working with your aunt and defended the baby." When she saw the picture, she recoiled to avoid the scene. Soff looked into it in detail.

When watching the slicing of the throat of the Negro, the mind of Soff retrieved his past experiences in the military as a Navy Seal. The technique was the same: piercing, deepening the blade, and slicing; all in one stroke. The cut had to be uniform in depth. As a medicine doctor who was to save lives, he felt uneasy having done so many kills. But as operational in special forces, he had to kill or be killed. The survival instinct overrules any command of conscience. He had received various commendations for his mission performances and good results. The ego expanded by the recognitions added to the survival instincts. Besides, his reasoning justified him when he saw that the enemies in Afghanistan and Western Africa did so many cruel things to innocent people. Now with Mariely, the baby child was taken away to do him God knows what. He was glad not to be called again for any of those missions. The State satisfied his special request of discharge with advantages, on the condition that he was kept registered for one year as a stand-by soldier, to be called if needed for special cases.

"Sir, sir, the lady here tells me that you are Doctor Soff," a foreign agent that arrived pulled him out of his distracting thoughts. His mind had turned to the past in a reverie of the memories of the beautiful and virginal Mariely.

"Hum. What? Who is asking?" said Soff. He turned and saw a partially bald man of over six feet, with a strong frame and a big jaw. The features of a devoted policeman of apparent service attitude but with the cold eyes of a killer. Soff saw some of his own traits in the man.

"I am Hancock, special agent for family affairs. You have been referred to Interpol by the Department of State of the USA to deal with a home affair related to a co-citizen of yours. You are to represent the person, a lady in this case, and investigate the criminal matters related to her case."

"Oh, Jesus. What the Department of State of USA wants me involved with and who made the request?" asked Soff.

"Let me clarify. The request is not from the Department of State. It is from the Navy Seals of the Department of Defense and the final recipient of the services is Interpol. Their problem is that the victim is Spanish speaking and will need somebody able to speak the language. Interpol would have to hire a translator but the pandemic of Covid 19 prevents it by budget and by persona. The National Central Office in Puerto Rico was consulted and they recommended you. They understand that you are the only one available capable of working the case with ease."

The agent's clarification led Soff to feel a hunch that led him to an insight that was shocking. It was almost disturbing. That was not a possible coincidence. He was afraid to ask but had to.

"Can you give me more details?" asked Soff.

"Sir, I do not have access to the details. All are included in this sealed envelope. You may tear the seals and see for yourself." Soff frowned while taking the envelope.

"Hum. Why so much confidentiality for a family affairs case? There is nothing extraordinary in this case. I mean, as related to national security."

"Sir, I do not have the slightest idea as to why this case demands so much attention and care. I just follow the orders to come here to deliver the documents. I came from London with the assistance of the National Central Office. I have to add that you should be in London as early as possible. I am sorry for the short time notice. Those were my instructions. I presume that abductions demand quick action."

"They are right. I need to see the scene immediately. As soon as I get to London. Did they isolate the scene?"

"They did, sir and there are officers guarding it around the clock. You'll see."

"I'll go home to get ready. Are you coming along?"

"Yes, sir. I'll be your company. You will not have to buy tickets. I got them here for you and they are confirmed. We are cleared to go through all the gates at the airport directly into an Airforce plane. I got orders to return with you."

Soff turned to the side, "Mariely, good bye. I have to go with this gentleman." Avoiding to give more details as was the discipline when he had assignments in the field. He got closer to her and whispered in her ear. She nodded in agreement, confirming she understood what he said. He walked away from her, this time speaking louder, "Remember to do as told. I hope that you are well when I return. Don't worry too much. Count on me and lean on God." Now turning to the agent, "Let's go, man." He had noticed the woman in his younger years and had a crunch with her. Pity that Gerard had her first. His failure was that he never expressed his interest in her because he would be overseas in the military. But still, he liked her. If she accepted him, he would be hers. The baby was no problem. He could raise him as his.

===

Soff and Hancock took off to the airport right after the doctor dumped five clothes changes in his military bag. Skipped the bath to save time to get to the airport to catch the plane. Hancock was ready; he returned with the same travel outfit. The trip was comfortable to the East London airport. From there his final destiny was the National Central Offices which was linked to Interpol. Via the Internet, they transferred him dossiers of criminals and abductors of children which he read in the cab. The criminals used to, mostly, kill the children and let them be a piece art of the scene. This meant that the child, for the time, was alive. The grimy thing was that this child was taken. When they took children, most of the groups practiced satanic rituals sacrificing them to make spiritual requests to evil forces. These groups were particularly fanatic and imposed their beliefs with extremes like killing and burning in dramatic ways: decapitation, burning alive tied to a post, and tearing the body's extremities. As long as a sacrifice spilled blood, it was the right one. Soff felt pity for this child of the case, being fragile and vulnerable, who could become a victim in the hands of these *trolls*. His thinking raptured him into considering that the child could be Mariely's. But he could not connect the situation in London with her. He had always liked the girl. On introspection, he had to admit that he thought frequently of her even while on the battlefield. His expectations were to marry her when returning from the military though he had never said a word to her. He had not thought that frequently of a woman. His thinking was interrupted when the cab stopped and rang the fees for the trip. "We arrived. Here's your National Central Office," said the cab driver.

"Let's hop out. They are waiting for us, Doctor Soff." Both started walking to the Office.

"OK. Here we go. I hope I can solve this case quickly. I was already spoiled in my place."

"Yep. Let us hope WE solve this case quickly. I am part of the equation, too. I am your assistant." Climbing two steps to guide Soff into the Office. "I, too, want to be free to enjoy my newborns. I got twins."

Soff widened his eyes. "Then you should not be in this case. You should be with your family. Seriously. I can take care of myself. Go back to your wife and sons." He stopped in the middle of the stairs.

"I volunteered. I know what we are to face. It is me the one who can help you," said Hancock.

"What do you mean?" asked Soff.

"I am aware that we are to confront spiritual forces. Both of us can handle that. Because we come in the name of God. Satan had been already defeated. We will be against Satanists."

"This is still dangerous, my good Hancock," said Doctor Soff. "Now, let us walk into the Office to get briefed and start our action."

As soon as they walked in, there was an officer who took care of the briefing and took them to the crime scene. At the scene, they made all kinds of observations. The concern of Interpol was because the cases of abducting children have increased to twenty times what used to be with an increase in killing them.

The various drops of blood led to DNA analysis, stains to search for compatible fingerprints, a piece of cloth led to searching the vendor and leftovers of food and music CDs, and forgotten toothpaste to the habits of the abductors. One of the abductors was careless and went into the apartment with dirty shoes leaving behind prints of his shoes.

They left so much evidence that Soff became suspicious. He turned to Hancock.

"There are so many evidence details that it seems that the abductors want to be found," said Soff.

"I have the same impression," said Hancock. "This is very suspicious. We have to be very careful. This could be a setup."

"Agree. We shall be careful," said Soff, then added, "Do you notice that nothing of the child was left? There is no pacifier, bottles, blankets, clothes, or pampers, child soap and wiping paper are gone. Yet I can see a strand of hair in the crib. It is gray hair. Obvious that these are mature people. This makes me think about them. Probably, most of them are grandparents. If they are, the situation makes them think about the suffering of the parents confronting the abduction of their kids. Like it would happen to their sons and daughters. If there is a burden of empathy, we have a great advantage. I would not expect callousness from a grandparent, thinking about grands of mine. We can use that sensibility to our benefit."

"How?"

"We will need the assistance of the press contact of the Office. Is there one? And, do you know who is?" asked Soff.

"It is a woman. I know her. She was my fiancée," said Hancock. "She will cooperate with our case."

"You don't need to elaborate on details, please. Just ask her to meet me so I can discuss my strategy with her," said Soff.

"Can I be present?" asked Hancock.

"Of course."

Two hours later the three were meeting to discuss the strategy of Soff. Once all was agreed, Hancock's ex-fiancée contacted the press. A week later, seven children were returned to the authorities with discreet anonymity. But how to determine whose mother is each? Fortunately, with the DNA analysis, there was no need to resort to the Moses crude solution of slicing the baby in two halves. Considering the parents to whom a child had been stolen, the tests were conducted and all was settled within three days. In three weeks Soff was back in Puerto Rico. He went directly to Guayama. The next day he visited Mariely which coincided with the moment in which her baby was being returned to her and laid on the crib by her side. Cooing him, he was aslept quickly and almost immediately she followed. Hancock was with him for the closure of the case. Watching the scene, Soff took the babe from her lap and placed him into the crib. On the bed, she looked unconscious, relaxed after getting her son back and out of danger. He went to his work at the nurse's counter. There he filled records and issued treatment orders for the patients. He remembered issuing orders for a relaxant for her to help to overcome the tensions of the abduction and reduce her swelling. Deciding to do it personally, he got up, got the medications from the drug dispenser, and went to see her.

The baby was not in the crib, and she was not on her bed. He supposed that she had taken the babe and gone to her home. *I cannot believe she is ungrateful and left without notice. Maybe she is getting even like when I left for the military.* So, he went back to the dispenser and instructed him to deliver the drugs to her home. Three hours later, when the delivery man returned, he informed me that neither of them was at home.

Soff decided to wait till the next day to confirm. It was the same: both had disappeared. This time he called Interpol to make the Investigation to avoid conflicted interests. Hancock was appointed with a local veteran, ex-green beret. The first point to investigate was the residence. There, a Californian immigrant who lived next door informed that Mariely had not been at home for days.

"You should look for her at the Hospital. I presume that she is with the kid," said mister Wendel. "Can I learn why you are looking for her?" Bending his head to the side he showed surprise, "I don't think that she had done wrong."

When five days passed, Soff started getting desperate. By the seventh day, he could no longer bear the waiting and decided to expedite matters. He was worried for the baby and the mother. His imagination and daydreams revolved around the mother. With some fantasizing about sharing intimate life with Mariely. He felt that the attraction was evolving into another affection that he had never felt before and he could not understand. He felt a strong attachment to the woman that he could not and did not want to avoid. That feeling produced in him a strong empathy for her suffering for the baby with him suffering it, too.

His feeling and the sinister circumstances of her abduction aggravated him deep within. He could not understand how this was going inside him but the feeling was there. Never before had he had those sensations with turmoils in his head and his insides. She was a need to appease a pain in his groin. He needed to find Mariely and her son. He had to take his own steps to get quicker results.

On the seventh day, he went to the house of Mariely to do a detailed examination of it, combing every inch of it looking for leading hints that could give some light for a direction to follow to solve the abduction. He will share his findings with Hancock. When he finished, he called Hancock to meet separately from the local veteran, the green beret Alcides.

When he met with Hancock, the latter showed him two pictures left by the abductors. Mariely and the kid were on these. Somebody was holding a sharp blade on the neck of Mariely, cutting a little on her throat, enough to make it bleed. Her tears rolled while looking to the left side. Another picture showed an ice pick pointing to the right eye of the child. In his innocence he smiled, playful with his hands trying to touch the pick. The baby was on her left side. Soff was shocked and remained almost mesmerized by the images while an intense almost blinding hatred arose in him. He controlled himself but Hancock took notice of his reaction.

You have to stay controlled," said Hancock, "The purpose of these pictures is to get you off rational balance. If you do not recover, they will win. If you play cool, they are bound to lose this war. We have to win, for the sake of Mariely and the child. I will get permission so that you can join with Alcides and me."

"Be ideal if you can get that permission, Hancock. I am ready to work. Let me share with you what I found in the house of Mariely." Soff proceeded to give Hancock his findings, things that eluded the examination of Alcides and Hancock.

Hancock was amazed at the additional information from Soff. The abductors were five. One of them was left-handed, wearing a cheap ring. One of them is probably black.

"How can you determine that?" asked Alcides.

"One of them picked the baby from the crib and pulled a string of thread from the mattress cover. There are footprints of the working boots usually worn by Negro laborers. This is a rare association free of racial prejudices like in the Satanist groups. That means that we have to hurry to rescue them. How are we to rescue them?" asked Soff with a frown. "We need to get to the group. Could somebody among your people identify organizations with mixed races, particularly with Negroes and Whites?"

"Are you serious? There are so many in this country. We don't hold so much of a grudge against black people. They are mixed everywhere with everybody," replied Alcides.

Soff observed, "Then we should be searching in high levels of management. The participants of Satanist cults are people of sophisticated education. Historically you could see this with Judas."

Hancock was quick to correct, "Wrong argument. Matthew was a doctor. Paul was of high class and with a very high level of education."

Offended, Soff corrected, "No. This is a reasoned argument. Doctors were educated with practice, not with sophisticated classroom teachings. Paul had a sophisticated education and was of high class but he was directly confronted on his way to Damascus."

With an appeasing tone, Alcides commented. "Hancock, I believe that we better agree. He is right. Let us do the assignment that he is asking from us." Alcides had the looks, with his sturdy body, of a cop.

Searching with the criteria for high levels, the assignment was done in one day. Quickly the trio went to visit the identified organization to assess their understanding. They confirmed the suspicions of Soff. The next step was to spy and find out where the kidnapped ones were and that they were alive. The next morning, they cleared all their doubts, located the place, contacted the police, and assaulted the place to rescue them.

They had a new surprise. Mother and son were not in the place. A note was left.

> "Next attempt to rescue the martyrs, their sanctity will be accelerated. You will be trapped and their execution will be in your presence. Then you will be executed by immolation. Do not force the situation. They will be sacrificed to the spirit of Tammuz. We went to England."

When Soff read the note, his face turned ashen. He could not, despite his embarrassment, hold his cry with a painful lamentation.

His was a cry of a condemned man. Tears flowed on his cheek. His were hot tears that rolled shamelessly. Like a madman, he vented his feelings aloud. He did not want to put up drama but he did not understand why he was carried away. The emotions displayed were very intense. This was embarrassing, but he did not care. He wanted to let this go out of his chest. The feeling was now sincere. It was, for real, burdening his heart. He felt impotent.

"How could this happen to me? God, why do you save me from wars and deprive me of the woman that can make me happy? If she is not the one, why do you let me feel like this for her? Don't you advise that man and woman should join? Why this is in my heart? Sunrise and sunset by her side will be my plenitude and you are taking that from me. I cannot bear it. Will you bring me death, also? Living without her is dying. Oh, God."

Hancock came closer to him and whispered, "Doctor Soff, hold yourself. By reacting like this you are showing that you are very vulnerable. There could be people around interested in assessing how easily they can control your will. Besides, you are defeated without even starting the fight. Clear your mind. There is a lot of work to do and a lot of risks to take. Come with me. Emotions are not to run you."

Alcides stayed away from them.

Hancock's consoling advice confirmed the good effect of his display. His courses on drama while he was studying for his master's came very handy. When he had used those skills, his enemies were fooled and he could accomplish his missions. This case is no exception. He has to admit that his emotions flowed sincerely to his surprise. All that he had were spurts of sincere emotions though his intention was to play with the emotions of others.

Hancock was disturbed by his dramatic reactions, but he had knowledge that added perspective to the situation, and he shared it, "Soff, in the note that they left, the Satanists have scheduled the sacrifice to favor the spirit of Tammuz. That happens in the middle of June. We have three months to find the mother and the child. It will not be easy for these Satanists to hide when they have to take care of a child. Besides, she is an intelligent and courageous woman. I bet that she will find a way to give us a hint as to their whereabouts. Cool down and think. Reason out the situation considering that we have three months to work."

"OK. I'll be more patient. Let us work on finding them. Alcides, will you help?

"Certainly."

"Then the first thing to do is locate secret organizations in town or close to town. Ask for a breakdown of ethnic composition. Ask also for their addresses, electronic or mail. Use any media that may result. Be comprehensive. After you get that, Hancock and I will visit their Negro members."

Alcides did his assignment in every detail and quickly the pair went out to visit the Negro members. Two months and a half passed and they did not have revealing results from any of the houses in the city. When they went to visit the suburbs, they found a house where the Negro was a mature man, his hair already gray. A preadolescent granddaughter received them.

"Grandpa, here are two men dressed in coats who are asking for you." Addressing Soff and Hancock, the girl said, "Daddy is not here. Are you from the office of family matters? Are you coming to take home the child that my father found?" Her grandfather arrived at the door.

Soff and Hancock played cool. The old man asked, "Can I help you, gentlemen?"

"I believe you can," said Hancock. "Are you a relative of the man of the house? Your name, sir?"

"Simone is my name, sir"

"I am Soff of the Special Forces and this here is Hancock, from the Interpol in England." Nodding, Soff went on with the subject. "We are looking for an abducted male child, white, and his mother.

The child is a baby. She is a young woman of around 27 years. The girl here says that her father found a child. Can we take a look at him? Is by any chance the mother of the child in here, too?"

"Yes; you can see the child." Signaling the men to come inside. "Follow me." He kept on talking. "I advised my son to take the child to a hospital to avoid problems. But his work routines don't give him much time. Some friends will join him to act as witnesses and then take the child to the hospital. The child is in the guest room. We don't hear him cry, though. We hear him cry during the night. A couple of days ago, a young woman came asking for the baby. My son told her that the baby was sleeping and to come back for him in the morning. His attitude was rude. There was another man behind her; this was a friend of my son and his wife (I have seen them a few times here). I guess that she got scared and decided to come back in the morning. She came in the morning at which time three friends of my son took her away. She has not shown up again to ask for the baby." Simone opened the door to the room of the baby who was cooing. "Strange mother she is. Must be one of those cases of unwanted pregnancies."

"Strange she is; no doubt," added Soff. Hancock nodded in agreement while going to the cradle to pick up the child. On the way to the room, he unscrew the cover of the phone mike on the living room table and inserted in it what looked like a coin. Quickly, he picked the baby and went out. Alcides was coming in.

"Alcides, how did you come to know that we would be here?" asked Soff.

"Well, basic. Weren't you looking for the child?" asked Alcides while pulling his gun from the right side holster and tapping the one on the left. He was looking straight into the eyes of Soff.

"What is wrong with you, man?" asked Hancock with his eyes almost popping.

"Nothing. He is one of the gang of Satanists," said Soff. Then BANG! A shot was heard. Soff looked at the gun of Alcides. It was not smoking, but the gun of the old man was. Alcides fell wounded. Soff took his weapon.

"What have you done, sir?" asked Soff, who was concerned with the girl. "Where is the girl?"

"Do not worry about the girl. I signaled her to go to her room," turning his head to point in the direction of the room, "to keep her out of this scene."

"Why did you shoot Alcides?" asked Soff. Hancock with his lips a line and his eyes popping.

"I am fed up with those sacrifices of children. Shooting him will cost me my life or, at least, the rejection of my son Valmides." Simone was still processing thoughts in his head; lowering his head in meditation, he added. "I have to protect my granddaughter and take a stand against these people. What they do is infamy. I would rather see my son Valmides trafficking drugs, despite it being another infamy. But the ones who consume can decide to do or not to do." Alcides was starting to move. "I will tie the bastard. You get out of here. I will stay with him and extract where they have the woman. He is in a high level of the Satanists organization. Save the baby. Get him out of here. Forget the rest." After a pause, he added, "Do not fear for the mother. They will not sacrifice her until they have the baby. Both have to be sacrificed simultaneously for they want to honor the spirit of Tammuz. Their petition is special which demands the spill of blood. I heard them say so. Now go."

Alcides was groaning with pain; he had a bullet in his torso. It passed him through. Simone tied his feet to his back with his hands while laying on the floor. The pain and the tying would not let him move. Simone probed into his wound with a surgical palette to increase the pain and inquire about the site of the woman, Mariely. After repeated tortures and more bleeding, Alcides was willing to talk. Simone passed the information to Soff. Shortly after, Alcides fainted for the bleeding and the pain.

When Valmides arrived he scolded Simone for freeing the baby and shooting Alcides.

"Father, Alcides is the head of my cell of Satanists. We are striving to put order in this world. That is why we need to make these sacrifices. The spiritual world gains strength from them. When it is mother and son at the same time, the spiritual world gains double strength and there is power to spare into our purposes for peace in the world." Valmides shut up, waiting for the ideas to sink into Simone's head.

"What power is it that you need for your purposes?" asked Simone.

"Forget that," replied Valmides. His tone was rough and disrespectful. His father coiled his attitude and retreated to the room of his granddaughter. He felt like a snake ready to strike whatever threatened his child. His only thought was: *Innocence should be protected at all costs.*

Meanwhile, Valmides, servile, freed Alcides from the tying.

"Does your father know the consequences of what he did? Would he be willing to yield his granddaughter and his daughter-in-law as replacements for the woman and the child that we had? Those are your daughter and your wife. What are you going to do? Remember that it takes centuries to have the gift that we have. It will take another century to have a child born in the day and hour of Tammuz and from a mother of spiritual attributes." A threat in his words.

"I will do nothing. I gave my oath at the initiation and I shall keep it."

"We allowed these rich people of Puerto Rico to believe that the sacrificial ceremony will deliver Gerard to the woman who wants to get pregnant by him. We are charging good money to her," said Alcides. "Let us first try to recover the child and prevent these Interpol men from getting the woman, the mother." But he did not confess that had given the whereabouts of the mother when Simone tortured him. Simone had been crudely cruel and was about to kill Alcides.

"Good for the money. Will I get some?" asked Valmides.

"You will get all for being the host of the baby," said Alcides. "You will get more money now that the woman thinks that she can be the bride of Satan and get all the treasures that she yearns to have. She is into all this for money. We are into it for the spiritual ruling. Within 28 days we should celebrate the ritual of sacrifice adoring Tammuz." His mind explored his thoughts before letting them out. "On the 29th day, we can be sacrificed by Tammuz if we have not complied with his wishes. We will be at the hands of Morgana, the priestess of Tammuz. We have been warned that there is no appeal if we fail and they sentence us to death. We will be declared martyrs. We will be the substitutes for the child and the mother."

"What are we going to do?" asked Valmides.

"First of all, kill your father," answered Alcides. "He is the one that freed the child and the Iofficers. Then, we may have to kill your daughter and your wife."

"What are you saying? "Valmides asked widening his eyes. "Are you crazy? How are you going to propose to me to kill my wife and my daughter and my father? They are close kins. You… we have to consider other alternatives.

"What I am telling you is what will happen. Not that I will do it. But somebody will be ordered to do it by the cloak of Tammuz," said Alcides. "Let us get out of here to look for the Interpol and the child." Looking Valmides straight into his eyes. "Are you sure that the woman is secured?"

"I do not know, really. Michael is taking care of that detail," said Valmides.

"Well, call him and ask him if she is at her home or some other place," said Alcides.

Valmides made the phone call and asked for instructions on how to get to the woman. Soff and Hancock heard the conversation and went to the city station to get a local cop to guide them to the address where the Satanists were keeping Mariely. During the delay in getting the cop, Valmides and Alcides arrived. Alcides shot them when they were going into the house. The bullet ricocheted on the column at the entrance. Two more men were in the house but Hancock and the cop shot and wounded them. Both laid on the aisle; one by the door of the room where they were keeping Mariely. He was bearing a mocking smile of triumph. Soff went fast into the room. They had her tied with chains and cuff links to a steel chair. Her mouth was gagged with a piece of thick cloth. Under her was a bomb C-4 with a timer. The clock was set to spark in fifteen minutes. Soff tension went up. He was hearing the shooting and the yelling. Two more men from the Satanists joined Alcides and Valmides. Soff hollered the cop.

"McKane, Do you have experts on explosives at the station?"

"We do, sir. I have to call them. But will they be able to come through the shooting?" Looking at the timer. "There is not much time to cope with the shoot-out and the C-4, though," said McKane.

"Call them in. We must handle the shoot-out on time." Soff walked out of the room. "Otherwise the whole block will be gone and us with it. Leave her gagged. Otherwise, her yelling will distract us in the shooting. Get the names of the men that were in here."

When Soff was walking out, he sensed a bullet singing by his ear. That meant that somebody was in a higher location. He hid behind the column of a window and peeked with a shiny pan from the kitchen to locate the shooters and described their positions to Hancock and the cop.

"No shooting. Let us play cool and save ammo. After twenty seconds they will get nervous and come out of their hiding to explore. Even then, do not shoot." Turning to the cop. "McKane, they do not know your voice. Change your clothes with the most fitting one of the men on the aisle. Holler to those outside that you have shot the three of us while distracted. We will do some shooting to simulate. Say that we lay wounded on the aisle. As soon as they come out, we shoot them."

"But they are four. We can hit three on time. What about the fourth one?" asked Hancock. "We should hit first the one with the machine gun but I do not have his precise location. Will you be able to hit that one on time?"

"No there is no area in here to roll myself. Besides I have to hit Valmides in particular while you hit the others. I have to locate that target and hit him to wound not to kill. At that time I can be the victim of the man with the machine gun. I have to hide real quick to avoid him. That would leave him free to hit me or hide to call more friends and the C-4 will get active."

"What? We have C-4 in here?" asked Hancock.

"Enough to blow a block and make a very deep hole," said Mckane.

"Holy," said Hancock. Now he was cold and frowning. "I never expected this to go to those extremes. I am glad that we left the child at the station with the social services woman. One less thing to worry about. Let us get the gears going. Time for action."

McKane did as advised by Soff. They had their locations and could shoot with precision. Each shot one of the men. Soff shot Valmides on the shoulder. He grossly fell to the ground. Soff did his best, hid on a column, rolled on the ground, and aimed to shoot the man with the machine gun. It happened to be Alcides. The latter raised the AK, and Soff was an easy target. He was ready to pull the trigger, with a happy cruel smile, then CRACK! It was a powerful shot of an explosive bullet. His head burst spreading gray and white greasy matter. His body thudded on the ground. He was dead. Simone showed by the side of the body with his long gun. Soff raised, gun in hand pointing to the floor. All was over. "I wounded your son to put him out of combat. If he kept shooting he could have been killed. He is a good man. You should all get away from this country.

A good place to raise your granddaughter could be South or Central America. Fly to the middle of the States and I'll get you documents to fly south of the border. Take good care of her," said Soff, and turning to the other officers, "Hancock, McKane, let us go."

The ambulances and a police car arrived and the expert in explosives deactivated the C-4 bomb. The first aid men took Mariely to the hospital. Hancock accompanied her. The wounded Satanist was taken in a second ambulance. Soff rode with him for interrogation. With his questioning, he got revelations of the places of group meetings. This information he passed on to Interpol for future action. He wanted to get out of this entanglement and live in another country.

When the two ambulances arrived at the hospital, Soff went to see Mariely. Before he opened his mouth, she spoke with her spontaneous attitude.

"Hancock told me all you have gone through and your loud crying for me and my son. I have to confess that in the past you had my attention but, out of respect, I was shy to show my feelings and interest in you. The reason that I was with Gerard was that you never showed interest in me and you went for military duty without saying a word. Seeing you at the hospital with the other doctors was a new hope for me. I hid my feeling because I was afraid of your rejection. But when I learned all that you had done, it is not hard to love you. If you are interested, I am here for you. I do not want to join any other man. You, I can trust. And love."

Soff lowered his head and talked not looking to her.

"I was afraid of falling for somebody at a distance and discovering unfaithfulness at my return. My hesitations led to the situation that we had now. This will never happen again. I want to join you. If you feel well, go take the baby and let us go back home." Raising his head and looking at her in the eyes. "I presume that Hancock will take care of all the reports. Hancock is taking care of your aunt. When he went to check at Alcides's residence he found her in the basement. Let us be for ourselves now." Later they joined and made love.

The Young Witch
By Pedro J. Ramirez

At her young age, Carla never expected to experience a dead of a close relative and much less holding death. She was sitting on the floor with the head of her brother on her lap. The living room was in disarray, as usual, with that strange violet tablecloth with dark stains that the visitors took for a sloppy print decor. The lamp, even on this spring day, gave a gloomy light, more like a shade. The wallpaper was of a brownish color, as selected by Carol, her sister, because she wanted it to be different like different was the way she clothed and clothed the table. Her brother Toñito was dead. He was killed by a man called Reuben—she took care of memorizing his name. He walked in with a man called Joseph and another that looked foreign and his accent evidenced it. But Joseph behaved with good manners and was gentle. Reuben was rough and produced a negative impression with his obvious lack of hygiene. In his rudeness, he shot her brother. A whim. No need for it at all. Sobbing, she held her brother, desperately wanting him to live, maybe resurrect. He didn't deserve to die. So young. Twenty-two years. The spilled blood clung to her pants as a sticky reminder of the violence. The foreigner felt a crush on Carol, her sister. Joseph kept him at bay but had to go out to keep watch on the neighbors. While he was out, the foreigner, Petrov, took the opportunity to rape her. She resisted the attack but he beat her to unconsciousness. She was penetrated rudely by the young thug. When she recovered, she was in pain and bleeding in the middle. Carla was forced to look at the scene, adding this pain to the loss of her brother. There were no more emotions to come from her. She felt like a stone. Tears rolled on her cheeks but on a face of no feelings.

It was too much to express and too much pain to hold. *Poor of my sister. She had been very jealous of her virginity.* When the bastard came, he spilled it on her face—to avoid getting her pregnant—smiled sarcastically, and called her "whore." She was a living insinuation. Then the man added: "Now you are ready for business. You look good. You can make bundles of money. You will make a beautiful whore. Marcell will give special credit to your mother. You will pay for your mother's use of heroin. Now wash and get dressed and don't say I raped you. Keep your mouth shut about this or I'll manage to kill you."

When Joseph returned and learned what had happened, he pulled his gun to kill Petrov. Reuben prevented it and hollered for all to move out fast. The men quickly grabbed the girls, tied them together, and got them and the body bag into the SUV idling outside. Carol was half dressed, one of her breasts almost showing and the cleavage on her rear exposed like a money slot. A luring coin holder. Her brassiere was scarce and transparent, her pants almost the size of her panties. She glanced furtively toward Joseph and felt shame. Once in the SUV, she had thoughts. *I wished Mother had never taken us along with her to visit Luigi, the narco dealer. His boss saw us and got struck by our looks. He told Luigi. Then problems exploded. Trying to protect us against a man with a gun at the door, Toñito was shot. Poor brother. What destiny are we going to have? Carla, oh, what is to be of her? The capo wants to take her. There's no way to fight these people. They are so powerful and they are armed. Oh, my God; Pa and Ma, what will they do when they learn about this? Who is this Joseph? I like him. He protected me... or tried to. Shit. On my hymen ripped condition I should not even think of a possibility. I don't have any more to feel after all this.* Both girls were like robots when the ruffians got them into the SUV. Their attractive bodies meant nothing; they did not feel. They could not offer the pleasures of young women of good looks. Semi-catatonic. They were like unemotional ragged dolls staring into the void. All the senses gone.

===

Forty-five minutes before and while the parents were at work or about to come out, late in that afternoon, thugs knocked on the door that Toñito opened, expecting to see his mother returning from work. When he noticed these, he opposed their entrance. Reuben used to act with violence and a man of scarce thinking, shot Toñito. When he bent down to avoid the bullet, it hit him on the forehead.

Five miles from home, the awaited-for-mother, Maricarmen, had detoured to see Luigi, the dealer, to get a sniff of heroin. Luigi stopped her on her way to the corner of sales and nodded her to go aside. He was a strong man with a hairy chest who always carried a gun.

"Why did you stop me, brother?"

"You have serious problems. The last time you came in you came with your girls. Big mistake. Marcell the bichote saw them and he is interested in them. He wants them for his parties. He is a pedophile and he liked your younger. Has a crunch with her. All the time he kept talking about her beautiful rear and her shape. Better for you to move out of the neighborhood. Go as far as you can."

"I will not relocate. That would be accepting his power over me and my family. That is not possible. I will not yield to his whims. Now it is me going away, what will it be later?"

"He is a very dangerous man… and very unscrupulous. Even people in my low world see him as rotten. Nobody likes him. The men that were under his pay last year saw him so rotten that they quit him. He recruited perverts like him. You should go. I insist."

"I won't go. Give me the dose I need for a sniff." Then looking into her shoulder bag for the money.

Grabbing a couple of bags, he said, "Here, have it. But don't blame me for what will happen with this Marcell."

"Don't worry. I will not." She spread the dust on her makeup mirror, took a long sniff, and left to go home. When she arrived home, none of her children were in. There was a bloodbath on the floor of the dining room.

"My God! What has happened here? Carla, Carol, where are you? Toñitooo. Come out. I am here." No answer. A note was left on the desk: 'They are mine now.' Nooo! This is not possible," she cried. Her desperate cry was heard by a neighbor at the next building, who came over.

"What's wrong?" said Fred.

"My daughters have been taken away. I think they wounded them; there's a blood pool on the floor. Tell me, do you have an idea of what happened here? Did you hear something?" He got pale and shook his head not wanting to say.

"I er, er. I heard a shot," said Fred, wrinkling his face.

"What? What are you saying? Did you call the police? Say, did you call the police?" she asked anxiously. "Oh, my God. My children."

"I did not. A man was outside of your home and threatened me with a gun making a sign of hushing with the fingers on his lips. There was nothing I could do at that moment. I am sorry, really."

"You are a coward. That's what you are."

"I am not. I had my children with me. I could not risk their lives with these men."

"Oh. I am sorry. I am so stressed. My children, my children. What will happen to them? I have to leave to find out." She left to see Luigi at the heroine sales corner. He was not there. She went to his home. His wife, a woman of dry skin with twisted lips, came out, confronting her.

"This is not the place of sales." She had a defiant look, her eyes clustered making a threat.

"I am not buying. I am looking for Luigi for information." Luigi came out of his room.

"What is your problem? You should not come to my home for any reason. Now, say what you have to say quickly and get out." He cooled when he saw the tears in her eyes. "What happened? What information do you want?"

"Need to locate Marcell and where he would take my daughters. I think that he killed my son. He was 22 years, young and handsome. He was my baby." She was under heavy stress, on the verge of crying. The breathing was heavy and sobbing in quick spurts. "I am bearing my suffering because he has my girls. Now I need to get my girls, my young babies. They are beautiful. They don't deserve what's happening. I want to get them back. Help me." Luigi looked at his wife, she had a face of compassion that erased her twisted lips.

"I cannot tell you. I risk my life and my family, you know how it is."

"A hint. Give me a hint and I'll do the rest. But I need to get to my girls."

"OK. Clearwater by the beach. That's all I can say."

"OK. Thank you. I'll find my way," leaving immediately in her Sentra. Luigi went back to his room and called Marcell, the bichote, from his international cellular. He explained with a shy voice the state of the woman and that she knew that he was at Clearwater.

On her way to see the bichote, Maricarmen stopped at the nearest gas station. Did all the vehicle checks for her long trip from Clayrmont and picked up the phone to call her husband, Marcos. She noticed then that there was a call from Carla. When pushing the receiving button, the voice in it was not Carla's. Some men were talking. But they were not talking on the phone. Their voices were distant. She heard Carla's and Carol's voices clearer.

Maricarmen heard her daughters and sent a buzzing signal to let them know that she was hearing.

Carla: "Uf. This place stinks like dead fish. Decomposed marine material."

Carol added: "Right on. The place and this company make you puke."

Both could not believe themselves. Their brother had been killed and they were talking trivia. But they realized that this was necessary trivia to signal her mother. They had to be rescued. If not, all would be for more suffering for Ma and Pa.

Then a man's voice hollered harshly: "Shut up or I'll slap you again. Want me to fuck you some more?"

Maricarmen didn't need to strain her imagination to figure out what was going on. *Poor of my girls. Facing a world like this.* The conversation went on with the man saying all kinds of blasphemies and indecent sexual proposals.

Carla: "Why did you have to rape my sister, brute? And then do it so brutally. You hurt her bad. Petrov is your name, isn't it?"

Petrov: "That's who I am. Petrov. Want me to fuck you so the sisters are ripped the same day? That could be your birthday celebration. You won't have cake but can have milk. All you want."

Carla: "Nothing to do in this place. Nice building but only for getting drunk and hearing stupid songs."

Maricarmen realized that the daughters were giving instructions to get to them. They were being defiant and at risk for giving away the location. Maricarmen had an idea of where they could be. She had gone to Clearwater Beach in the past summer with the family. Marcos wanted to go dancing but she didn't; she knew where was the dancing place at least. She worried for Carol. She was the older but was too temperamental and could upset this Petrov and cost her life. Or a repeated rape. *I cannot bear the thought of that. She is a good girl. Whimsy but good.* The instructions continued for a few more minutes. Petrov had the pronunciation of a foreigner. Easy to identify. The men never noticed that Carla's phone was ON. Carla asked permission to go to the restroom and Maricarmen heard an electronic hissing. *I think that she threw the phone in the toilet. It seems that her strategy was becoming dangerous. Smart, ah!* The mother had all the details that she needed. She needed to transform into her secret capacities. That was better. Calling Marcos could cost his life. She could solve the problem.

===

Maricarmen recoiled into her past and started some invocations and strange words. Her mind generated a fast-running picture of her past life. Her grandmother told her how they came to Puerto Rico through the stories of her grand-grandmother. They related to the queen of England in the peaceful use of witchcraft. They held meetings to make enchantments to prevent wars, genocides, make serial criminals surrender to the law, and work on the political scene to prevent conflicts among countries. The English queen realizing that persecution for witches was growing, secretly asked the queen of Spain—who discreetly was a practitioner—to take the grand-grandmother—in those times a witch in England—under her custody. At that time Puerto Rico was the best place to hide, in the mountains, among the still prevalent natives. The guild of witches was not ruled by political differences.

With years, the family expanded and adopted a Spanish name to avoid distrust and gain acceptance. With passing years, the guild of witchcraft grew in skills which they practiced secretly and decided to yield those skills to the descendants. So, the grandmother received those gifts and passed them to the mother of Maricarmen and the latter was, at this moment, the end of the line. Maricarmen envisioned passing the gifts to Carla in spite of being the younger. Carol was too temperamental and would give herself away and provoke persecutions. With the concerns for her daughters at this moment, the invocations kept flowing from Maricarmen with the strange witch language and she started feeling the powers, which had been dormant, reawakening. Her thinking and invocations have lasted the trip to Clearwater.

Her memories kept recurring out of chronology and becoming fresher: She remembered having pre-marital sex. She enjoyed it so much that decided to marry and get pregnant and then have three children. Only three. Before this, she was a practicing witch. Her powers matured with the practices that she had. So high were her powers that she was invited to lead the practicing witches of Occident. She refused and decided to live a normal life, away from the battles and persecutions of "witch hunters." This first sexual experience made her fall in love with Marcos. She had never experienced sex until she met him. She felt so delighted with the experience that she decided to live as a common person and married him. This conflicted so much with her powers that she started filling the voids of her yearnings for power with drugs. As the drug use increased, she became more dependent on it to escape her new reality of being a simple and powerless woman. Having experienced her great powers in witchcraft and the leader status recognized by her family of the craft, she felt that she had no way out. It was then that the relatives paid the price of her not-to-be-paid loans that she asked from them. Her husband complicated the situation. She was afraid that he would go, leaving her with the three children—already men and women—but she had alternatives. She had noticed that Luigi was falling for her. Relating sexually to Luigi was sports for her, not adultery. She felt no desire for Luigi or any loving. She acted out of convenience, like a real witch. In her mind this shocked her—she had an unemotional approach when facing particular situations. She felt extremely unemotional when facing threatening situations.

Her flow of memories interrupted when she was approaching the place. It was when she noticed three Escalades blocking the road. They were not the police or the army. She suspected something wrong and stopped her car distant enough from them—she could see them but stayed in the car far enough to force their initiative. They quickly showed initiative. They started with two shots in her direction and walked forward. The time had come for her to show her supernatural powers. She felt that the witch in her was alive again. The question that filled her mind was 'How did the people know that she was coming?'

They kept closing the gap toward her. Ten men were to intercept her with AK-14s, grenades, pistols with laser ray pointers, and knives. Marcell had given orders to kill her. This was, obviously, an overkill against an unarmed simple woman. The men surrounded her.

"Step out of the car," hollered Reuben.

"You moron. Out of what am I going to step?" she answered with a sarcastic tone. Smiling and saluting each with a nod. "You have seen this beautiful day but you will not see any more of it if you stay there. Better be gone. I'll count to three. One—" They started laughing at what they considered a joke.

"What or who will help you? You are dead meat, rotten dead. You look good. I wish I could fuck you but I have orders to kill you," said Casper, the second lead man, aiming at her.

"Two—"

"All of you, aim her and shoot when I shoot," ordered Casper. But when he was pointing at her, a strange force pushed his machine gun to the side. Now it pointed to the man at his right. "What the hell—"

"Are you out of your mind, Casper," cried another man at his left and raised and pointed the gun at Casper. By instinct, he looked to the sides and noticed that each man was pointing to his peer, each with eyes open and with his jaw down. Tense and amazed one of the men cried, "Are you all crazy?"

"Don't you see that you are crazy, too?" the man at his right asked, "You are pointing to Casper. Now he is pointing to you. What are you doing? What are *we* doing?"

"It must be because of that bitch. Must be a witch. Fuck. We are all going to die," said Casper.

"You will all certainly die if you don't go from here, NOW!" hollered Maricarmen. "See how it happens," making a swirling gesture. All the guns went up in the air shooting in all directions but them. Some bullets pierced the two Escaldes.

One of the men took the opportunity and pointed his laser gun to her but another hit him with the shoulder end of his rifle. "Fool! Don't you see that she could kill us if she wanted to? She is choosing to leave us alive. Are you stupid? Do you want all of us to die? Bastard!"

"You," signaling the one with the laser gun, "come here." He walked obediently to her. "You will take me in your car to Marcell." All the other men left. *Obviously, somebody told Marcell that I was coming for him. Nobody knew it but Luigi and his wife. But he's the one with the phone number. The snitch rat. I'll get back to him later.*

===

At the pub saloon, Maricarmen shouted, calling for her daughters. A man answered, gun in hand.

"There's nobody for you to call in here." It was the voice of Petrov. He had a strange accent which she recognized

"I know you. You are Petrov, right?"

"How come you know my name?" asked him with a shocked look.

"It's good to be sure that you are the man who raped my daughter."

"What? Ha, ha, ha. Would you like me to rape you, too? I can do it the same way. I guess she enjoyed it secretly. You are not a virgin; you can enjoy it freely."

"Son of a bitch. There's no way for you to reach me. You are to pay for what you did to my child. AND YOU WILL PAY NOW. Since you enjoy brutality, let's see if you enjoy it on you." Then she made some gestures, swirling her hands. His pants and underpants came down exposing his intimacies. Again, she swirled her hands and ordered, "Bend." His body curved from his waist pushed by a strange force. Then a swirl upward and the broom of the salon rose pointing the stick to his rear and thumped inside him penetrating very deep inside. With agonizing cries, he voided and excreted right there. He fainted and fell dead. With his cries more men came to attack her, gun in hand. The last one with a machine gun. This last one slid on the excrements of Petrov and started shooting involuntarily. With this, killed and wounded four of the ten running toward Maricarmen. The five remaining pointed at her and suddenly their guns went up in the air, floating and shooting but not killing. Maricarmen and the men were equally amazed. She was not doing it. *Carla must be the one doing it*, deducted Maricarmen. At the door of the room of prisoners was Carla, smiling at her mother.

"We can go, Mother."

"Not so fast," said Marcell, who showed up suddenly, pointing his gun at Maricarmen. She was not ready to react and he shot her, the bullet went into her right shoulder. Then, addressing Carla, "I don't want to kill you. My aim is perfect. What will you do, young girl? I like your courage. I'll make you my woman," said Marcell with a glee look appreciating Carla's shapes. But she produced gross news for him.

"You are late. I have been used by Reuben like Petrov did with my sister," said Carla with a mocking smile. "And he was not cruel, like Petrov. He did it well. You should congratulate him and Petrov for taking care of your women. Here look." Carla showed her panty with blood. It was a panty stained with the blood of her dead brother when she sat by his body.

"She's lying. She's lying. I didn't do it. I didn't touch her," said Reuben desperate, amazed that she displayed her panties, anticipating what would surely happen.

"She's saying it and I am seeing her blood." aiming at Reuben. The seconds of distraction was enough for Maricarmen to recover. Swirling her fingers, the gun in the hand of Marcell got hot and he could not hold it. Some more men came in but Carla gestured and their weapons went up in the air, shooting in all directions. Then the police showed up. All the men lay on the floor. All of them surrendered, including Marcell. All started explaining to the Police but the guards took it all as nonsense.

"Now we can go home," said Maricarmen. On the way out she got close to Marcell and whispered in his ear, "Now we are two against you. As time passes we will have higher powers. We may even visit you at the jail and show you some special powers. We will invite some sisters of the guild to make a real show that will drive you crazy. Expect it." Then, turning to Carla, "How did you learn what you did?"

"I started feeling strange and the things that I thought of started happening. I tried it by thinking little things against them and saw them happening. The guns in the air were the biggest thing that I thought and I saw it happen. Now you explain to me, Mother, what other big things can I do?"

"There's no limit, honey. There's no limit. Keep on experimenting." Carol heard and observed. She was not interested in those powers that could make her like a freak when people learned about them. She just looked around for Joseph. He was not among the prisoners. He fled on time. Good and bad. Pity.

===

A few months later Marcell was declared crazy and hospitalized for dementia. But he never recovered. Constantly, with a staring look, he claimed that he had visitors from the other world. On the other end, Luigi's customers were constantly finding a surprise when sniffing their drugs. The drugs had worms and a smell of rotten meat. With this, he could not sell the drugs to pay back the bichotes—the drug lords. He lost his business, ended in ruin, and was threatened for not paying his purchases. His wife left him with the children.

Maricarmen and her daughters lived well. Carla became powerful and reached a high position among the leaders of the Occidental Guild of Witches. Later, love knocked at her heart with a wealthy man. Her mother advised her to keep her powers a secret and to sharpen them to protect her family.

"Use the guild powers to protect your family. Nobody should hurt you," advised Maricarmen

Some months after the Clearwater confrontation, Carol was approached by Joseph who dismissed her shameful condition and she accepted him, married, and moved to Europe. The mother refused to use her powers and stayed with her husband, Marcos. No more sniffing. Young as they were, they decided to go for another child, and in two more years, they had another child, a boy. They called him Hidalgo to emphasize his future links to the high courts of the guild. He had the seed to be a warlock.

Salmonella
By Pedro J. Ramirez

It was a sunny Monday. It was spring. She got off the sheets to get clean. The room wallpaper was juvenile. It made the proper place for adolescents with hormonal rages anxious for quick sex. Her thighs felt slippery and sticky. She had a mixture of hers and his fluids.

"Michael, I have to go. The kids should be about to arrive on the school bus," said Andreina.

"All right. Will I see you tomorrow? I want to be with you. I want you to scratch my back with those long nails. I love that pain. It reminds me of your excitements and makes me relive and desire you more."

"I don't think so. Tomorrow will be a very important day for my husband. He will be in a commendation ceremony for the good job that he had done in his company. The whole family is expected to be there. Being a housewife, I am expected to be there," said Andreina, while rubbing her thighs with a wet towel to get dressed, "I'll call you again during the week." Now getting into her pants and blouse. "After I redo my nails. Next time I'll slice your skin so it gives you lasting pain and desires me more, ha ha ha. You are as good as I expected when I saw you the first time. And had been good all the time." Going to the door. "Goodbye."

"You are super. I feel you like no other. I feel your wants flow into me. Goodbye," said Michael still laying in bed.

He lost peace when she left. He felt a strong desire for her. He knew that she felt the same for him. He could not understand his feelings nor why she would go along with this play with three kids and a good prosperous husband. They have been in this game for three months. It was bad news that there was an emotional attachment growing stronger. He recalled when they met. It was while she was giving a Bible lesson.

The church classroom had thirteen kids. A year after, there were twenty-four. It was then that she was anointed to be like an angel guardian for the kids, helping them to grow spiritually. Then he was appointed as her assistant. She was very attractive and he had the athletic figure which the kids admired. She had black hair. Long. It made him imagine her breasts camouflaged by her hair. He would have to uncover them for caressing. Her breasts were abundant and firm but not bulky. Her hips made a soft wave that showed a tempting discreet femininity and a protruded oval at her rear. Her radiance was the killer: She enjoyed being a woman and showed it with the inviting curling of her lips when talking. He enjoyed being close to her and she enjoyed his playfulness with the kids. He could play with all the kids for exhausting hours without getting tired. She imagined him in another kind of play.

She imagined that he could be a continuous no-rest lover. Her husband never played with the kids and looked at them with his intellectual pose. They felt afraid that he would be Mr. Know-all, making all kinds of cultural questions. They enjoyed playing and joking. They had a lot of fun with Michael. She could not help having sensations in her body when he was close to her. Those were sensations she didn't feel for her husband. His lovemaking was routine-like, like a rational act for procreation as ordered by the Pope. He was a good performer but didn't do it with passion or desire. It was his "act." Just that. He didn't even show pleasure when doing it.

His "act" made her wonder what he felt when he was holding her in his arms when she did oral sex when she bit him, and scratched his skin when she was coming. He didn't display his emotions during those moments. This made her feel insignificant. His sex was an obligatory marriage activity that never included fun. Were it not because she felt the itch to be penetrated, she would not do it. There was no freedom of joy in him. He was so dutiful. Michael made her fly free into incredible pleasures and he demonstrated how much he enjoyed her. Her husband made her feel like a fly on the back of an elephant.

===

And so they enjoyed their adulterous sex relations; with great and deep satisfaction. She would not quit her husband because she felt she had too much to lose. Hendrick was a good man and was very generous. Besides, she had three kids who were her stars. At their ages, they were very mature. Tommy was smart and observant for his ten years. His language was adult-like when making observations. Timothy was very sentimental and fond of his father. Tim shared a great interest in history and followed his father's conversations on history with incredible lucidity for his nine years. Alice was the girl of Daddy. She was smart and was interested in the ideas of her father related to efficiency at work. She applied these ideas to her studies in her eleven years. The three of them had red hair and mild freckles, like Hendrick, which proved that the kids were his. They were very tender.

In spite of considering hers an ideal status in marriage and motherhood, she felt a powerful attraction for Michael and yielded to it. She could feel delights that she had never felt. Multiple times and with an incredible intensity that exhausted her into a state of complete relaxation. The pleasure was so much that it was almost painful. It was a sado-masochistic feeling. She never felt like that with Hendrick or any other of the three men with whom she had gone to bed in her youth. Michael was by far the greatest delight. These experiences made her feel like she was in a new heaven.

A Wednesday in summer, when coming out of the hotel pleased with her sexual experience of the day, an old lady addressed her. She had a wrinkled face with flesh strands that signaled her age. She was neatly dressed in a simple dress. She looked at her intently, like scrutinizing deep into her with her little piercing eyes. She was like a small totem of wisdom. Andreina had come out radiant. Her half smile showed her pleasure. The lady addressed her.

"You are more than satisfied with the time you spent in the upstairs room with him, don't you? Your satisfaction goes beyond human understanding," said the old lady, "because they are not natural. He is persuasive making you believe that this is a merge of souls that justifies your illicit relations. And you see with pleasure that something comes out of you into him. This makes you feel that your relationship has a deep spiritual meaning. Isn't that so? Tell me, woman."

"Yes, but how do you know all this?"

"The spirit of God is one and he wants you to know that he is watching you," said the Old lady, "The Spirit anointed you to be like an angel for the kids and make them of a higher spirit and you are not doing what is expected. I have been sent to you to give you the words. A warning. Be careful and do what the Spirit expects. You have to stop what you are doing. This man you bed with is not what you think. And, for him, you are not what he thinks. At both ends you go against kids by your mutual seduction. Beware. God will do justice. You are both under the whims of your feelings. The Holy Spirit is waiting for you to come and rely on Him. You have the doors opened for spirits of death and condemnation like Incubus and Succubus. These are for the death of kids. Both are acting against you. Remember, kids are in the heart of God. Beware and don't do what you are doing with this man anymore. You and him have been chosen. If you disobey, this will bring death. God will let Incubus and Succubus overtake both of you. You are more than him because you have been anointed. You'll be first. You'll suffer more."

===

Andreina went back home on time to meet the kids and, eventually, Hendrick. It was Wednesday and the local stores had special offers. On the way, she bought toys, pizza, ice cream, cakes, and dinner for all. That was a delight for them. But she kept on thinking about what the lady told her. She had a conflict but the debate in her mind was quickly solved.

How could I go against my kids? This lady is crazy. True, I am doing wrong but so many more do the same as I do and nothing goes against their kids. I don't think I should be afraid. Let me skip these thoughts. They are torturing and I don't deserve this. It is fastidious.

She dug into the pleasure of the cake and the ice cream and the incident with the old lady started to fade in her memory. But in an instant, she felt transported to a strange place. She had her eyes closed and had to strain to open them. She was surrounded by a multitude of penises and felt her body sticky. She touched and rubbed her skin to feel and see what she had on. The sticky substance was white and looked like the boiled starch that her grandma cooked for ironing the clothes but it stretched and made fine threads. Somehow she sensed the taste. It was salty and with a pungent smell.

"You want more of these? I can get you as many as you want. You want the thick liquid on or into you? All these dicks will come for you. Any time you want, but you are to refuse them for me," said a deep voice.

"Who are you?" Andreina asked.

"I am your most secret male. Call me Incubus," said the voice.

"What do you want from me?" asked Andreina.

"Don't you see why I offer?" asked Incubus. "I care for something else, the kids. I like to be surrounded by dead kids." Incubus pointed to a group of kids. They were all ugly and deformed, their hair was of fetid worms, freckles exuding pus, and their skin with stains and putrid sores.

"Aghh! That is horrible. What happened to those kids?" asked Andreina.

"They will have what you destined them for," said Incubus.

"How could I do something so horrifying?" said Andreina.

"What surrounds you?" asked Incubus. "Isn't it the way to sin? They have the consequence of your acts. Wait and you'll see what will happen." Andreina stirred her body like she had suffered an electric shock. Alice, Tim, and Tommy were in front of her.

"Mom, what's happening to you? You are like a mummy," said Tommy.

"Yes, mom. You look weird and shaky," said Tim

"Right on, Mom. You were like Melinda next door with her diabetes," said Angelica.

"Hush. Hush. Shut up. Don't say anymore. Your father is coming in here. This shall be our secret. Let's not worry about him," said Andreina. A few more minutes and Hendrick walked in. "Good evening, Hendrick. How was your day? In a minute I'll heat the dinner. It'll be Italian chicken, roasted center-cut ribs, corn cobs, vegetables, and smashed potatoes a-la creme so everybody is pleased. All are from your favorite restaurant, McSorley's."

"Great, let's eat," said Hendrick.

"I'll need to warm the food."

After eating and relaxing for a while, they showered and went to bed. After a short conversation on the events of the day, she covered Hendrick with her body and kissed him with a fictitious passion to which he responded with a powerful erection. She sat on him to make it go deep. She moved with rhythm feeling great pleasures. The rest was for his quick-coming pleasures. She had a hard time pleasing herself. She had to think of Michael. Later, when all was over and he slept, the vision came back to her. She had no explanation for it. She understood that it had to do with Michael, but could not understand the meaning of the whole scene. It disturbed her to think that there was something wrong with the kids, but her intelligence could not penetrate it. It was as if her intelligence had been short-circuited, as if her understanding was faded. She fell asleep and had another dream: Many kids went toward her with a menacing attitude. They had red, purulent eyes and their fingers were bones with pieces of rotten flesh. Their flesh came off in pieces when walking toward her. No word or noise came out of them. She awoke with a gasp, desiring to cry loud, but she bit her lips and saved the cry; she didn't want to give explanations. Her intelligence could not penetrate this second dream either. She felt void of reasoning.

===

After meeting on Friday and doing it a second time in the same week, Michael stayed at the hotel in bed for some more time. He reviewed in his mind the routine he and she followed to please each other. The sensations were good and intense. His and her comings were simultaneous. Once was not enough. Four times was right. More would be better but she had to go before the kids returned from school. She felt very satisfied each time he spilled inside her. He felt very satisfied when her comings spread warm on him. Her moaning and his grunts made a symphony of pleasures squelched by the steel strung of the muscular tensioning and release. They were a pair for each other.

Suddenly his thinking was cut. The images were not his. He was surrounded by a multitude of vulvae that dripped juices that swamped him. The juices covered him to his neck. The smell was intoxicating and, in spite of being engulfed by the liquids, he wanted more. Then a big vulva came to him with a soft and mellow voice.

"Do you like all this? If you want more," said the big vulva, "you can have all you want but you better not, for you are mine only. I am Succubus, you know me, don't you?"

"How come I should know you?" asked Michael in his trance.

"Every time you open your heart to the desires of your flesh," said Succubus, "you open the doors for me to visit you. Then you welcome me and get inside me with hard thrusts and empty your pleasure, with grunts and fatigue. How come you say that you don't know me when you have been inside me? I think I will drown and swallow you in pleasures"

"No, please, don't," said Michael, "don't do it, please, don't." Michael awoke with thick drops of sweat on his forehead. Last Wednesday he had a dream in which he saw many rotten kids towards him with their arms stretched to him and ready to strangle him. It was really horrifying. All was surreal and disturbed him. He tried, but could not understand what was in these dreams. Searching in his mind he could not discern the event nor come to a conclusion. The same lack of understanding happened with the Succubus vulvae that attacked him. He felt like a victim without a way out, thus he conformed and went along with the benefits of the pleasures. He could not help wanting Andreina more. Maybe he should control this but he got despaired like he never did. Being inside her made him feel like nothing else mattered. He felt doomed not to have her.

Michael was not interested in any other woman and felt that no other could satisfy him to the plenitude that she could. It was beyond his understanding. Succubus or whatever. He knew that he could lure other women. He had the looks to do it. But he was not interested in any other woman. Andreina was the one for him. But Succubus thought differently.

===

Andreina and Michael met again on Thursday the following week in a hotel room. It was 9:45 AM when they met. They shared dreams and visions. Discussing these, they decided to think about them deeply and look in their Bibles if there could be any revelation. They felt that their understanding was blackened; something was missing and they could not identify what. When they talked about the possibility of a revelation, a voice was heard.

"You will learn what is being shown with the dreams and visions at the proper time," said the voice. Both heard it.

"That's the voice of Incubus," said Andreina.

And another voice was heard: "You will learn what is being shown with the dreams and visions at the proper time," said the other voice. Again, both heard the voice.

"That is the voice of Succubus," said Michael

They felt afraid and embraced each other, her leaning on him. Being tightly close, the warmth of their skin started exciting them. Soon the voices were forgotten and they performed on each with great passion and pleasure. One, two, three times. Him inside her, they rested for a few minutes and did it again. One, two, three times. She felt exhausted and thirsty but desired to do it again. He was in a fever and ready to do it again. They could not understand how they could make so many repeats and be ready for more. They were in a marathon syndrome. Then she heard a whisper.

"Do more, do more, Andreina," said Incubus, "I want you to do more until you bleed."

Michael kept going on. Undisturbed. This day he had incredible stamina. He didn't bother to understand it. He just enjoyed it and kept going. After forty-five minutes, she was bleeding. He felt her warm wetness on his pubis and got more excited. She stopped and unclimbed and there was blood.

"Are you hurt? Did I get too deep? What happened?" Michael asked.

"There's nothing wrong and I feel OK. Too much OK. I would do more but I am concerned about the blood. You, too, are bleeding on your back, saw it when you turned. The new nails I got are too long and sharp. Be better if we quit now. We had done enough, more than enough. I lost count of my orgasms. Besides, I heard the voice of Incubus asking me to do more 'until bleeding'" She went to the bathroom and took a shower using cold and hot water. The bleeding stopped. She got dressed and left. He always kept watching her desiring more but she ignored it. She started to worry. Now, pulling her mind backwards, she recalled the conversation with the old lady three weeks ago. On the way back to her home in the Uber taxi, she meditated the conversation with the old lady. When she got home, decided to go to bed and take a nap to cool off and think to gain some insight. During the nap, there were no dreams, no visions. Maybe she was cured for sins are washed with blood and it was all over. But Incubus told her differently.

"Bitch, are you happy now? You never had done it so many times, right? Your bleeding is your sacrifice to me. You are on a pact of blood with me. How about that, honey? Now you are mine, mine, mine. You are not going to be with any other man. If you let any other man do it to you, I'll punish you." She overstayed in bed and called Hendrick asking him to bring dinner, claiming that she was not feeling well. She felt feverish with desire. She wanted Michael but Hendrick would do it if he felt like it. All she wanted was to feel a man inside her.

Time in bed passed quickly. The kids were in and she gave them some ice cream and cake and went back to bed. Shortly after, Hendrick arrived with dinner.

"Hon, you want me to heat dinner now?" asked Andreina.

"No, go back to bed. I have better plans. Let me take a quick shower," said Hendrick. He walked into the bathroom, showered, and came out to her, naked. "Now I want you for dinner, dear." Caressing, kissing, her all over. As soon as he felt her ready, got into her. Her moaning was deep as she came. This is when she heard the voice of the Incubus.

"I told you. I'll punish you. Wait and see. You don't play with me."

Ignoring Incubus, she kept on and came more times. Her orgasms were intense and in chains. Hendrick was very pleased with her responsive disposition and this prompted him to an orgasm with a deep and long grunt. They both slept for a while and fed the kids, who watched TV. Meanwhile, they enjoyed the bed some more. Hendrick was exhausted and pleased. Both had a light dinner and went to sleep.

Andreina thought about Michael. *Could he be having problems, too? He says he heard somebody, 'Succubus', he says. That is related to Incubus by what I heard at the Bible school. I don't understand any of this and I don't want to talk about this with anybody else, 'cause they would learn about me and him and the price would be too high for me. I guess the old lady is derailing and confused.*

Another day was gone and Andreina did not experience problems. She started feeling more confident that nothing would happen with the Incubus.

===

It was Friday. Breakfast time. Hendrick wants more of her. Her receptivity of last night excited him so much that he wanted to experience it again. She called his office to excuse him for a later arrival. Then hurried to the bathroom to pee and void. When wiping, she scratched her ass with the new long nails. She did a quick wash of her hands and went to make breakfast for the kids.

"Pancakes, Tommy?" asked Andreina. "Tim, pancakes. How about you, little girl?"

The three made a chorus, "Pancakes, Mom. Yes." All three ate well and off to school.

Now she was alone with Hendrick. He was waiting on the bed, ready for her. Feeling passionate, he wrapped her in his long thick arms and gave her a long tongue kiss. She had an outflow of wetness and felt sticky. He lay her softly on the bed and kept on kissing all over. Then got into her. Hendrick had never done it like that. They continued at the same pace and with the same routines of lovemaking for almost two hours. She was ready to feel more when she heard the voice of Incubus.

"I told you that I would punish you. Remember you are mine," said Incubus. "All that you enjoy now you will feel sorry for later."

"What did you say, Honey?" asked Andreina.

"Ma', how could I speeaak? Oh, Lord, I am coming. Cooomiing," said Hendrick, all in grunts. He was already empty. The phone rang.

"Who could be this early in the—," said Andreina.

"It's over ten O' clock already, Hon. We have had so much fun that I forgot that I had to go to the office. Maybe they are calling me. I'll answer."

"I'll wait for you. I want a 'goodbye' one. Can you do it for me?"

"Yes. We are connected like never."

She brushed off her sweat and noticed a strange smell. She examined her hands and noticed a spot deep in some of her nails. She went to the bathroom to wash her hands while Hendrick picked up the phone and talked.

"Hello. The school director? What? When did this start? Ten O'clock? OK, I'll pick them up. What now… at the Hospital. OK, I'll be there in twenty minutes. Hon, you heard. The three children are sick and had to be taken to the Hospital. Let's get it all under control before we do more fun. Clean yourself with a wet towel and get dressed, honey, let's go to the Hospital." Both got into the car quickly and arrived at the Emergency Room. The children were with high fevers, wet with perspiration, pale, and short of energy. Andreina worried. They had never been sick like that. She looked at Hendrick. Then she turned to the doctor.

"Can we take them home? I can take care of them."

"I'm sorry ma'am. I cannot let you do that. They are seriously ill and will need professional care," said the doctor, who was a specialist in pediatrics. "At the moment, even we are under a heavy burden by their state. You should return home and wait for our news. I anticipate that you should expect bad news more than good. Let us all hope that it will be for good news." They left the hospital in a sorrowful mood. They were very tired. Andreina asked Hendrick to make her company and not go to work. He stayed home. But no more fun. At night time, they sipped some wine waiting for news. No news. They decided to go to bed. Staying in peace they slept. At 4:23 AM, the phone rang. Andreina got up to answer and then heard Incubus.

"I told you I would punish you, whore."

"What?" asked Andreina.

"Ha Ha Ha Ha Ha," was the answer from Incubus. "I told you, remember, bitch."

Andreina picked up the phone. "This is the doctor from the Hospital. Are you a parent of the children Timothy, Tommy, and Alice of the Allen family?"

"Yes. I am her mother, Andreina."

"Well... I um... eh sorry to say that the three children... hum... died at 3:56 AM. My condolences for this hard moment. I am very sorry. We did all we could but suddenly all got out of control without logical explanation and they would not respond no matter what treatment we tried. Very sorry, ma'am. The whole staff offers condolences, too."

"Noooo! This is not possible," said Andreina, dismayed on the carpet. Hendrick woke annoyed by her scream. He noticed the phone off the cradle and understood what had happened. Andreina felt him lifting her and laying her on the bed. Shortly after, both got dressed and went to the Hospital. The three little bodies were laying one beside the other. Pale with a sanctum expression. She understood that this was the Incubus's revenge. Words choked in her throat; she would not say a word.

After realizing that they could not do much, Andreina and Hendrick asked the mortuary services to take care of the funeral. Then came back home. Andreina stayed mute. Home was so lone and empty. Andreina decided to go to her room. He decided to pick a book from the credenza. The phone light of messages was blinking. Who could be? I already called the office to take the day off. He pushed the play button. It was Michael.

"Call me back. I need to see you. Make the time. Will you?" He recognized the voice of Michael, the children's instructor at the church. His voice sounded with tones of intimacy and with the entitlement to demand her presence. He didn't like those tones and recalled the many times that he observed her close to Michael at the church. She never did this before. He pushed the button to retrieve the record of the calls made from Michael's phone. There were twenty-five calls in less than two weeks. He got mad, but being in the middle of his

children's decease, he decided to calm down and take an investigative approach.

===

Four days after burying her kids, Andreina felt crushed. What the autopsy revealed crushed her more. The intestines of the kids were swollen and sealed. "This was not natural," the doctor had said. "The symptomatic expulsions provoked by the salmonella bacteria should have saved them. But the sealed intestines made us at the hospital think that the illness was something different. We could not understand what was the illness and could not produce a diagnosis." The doctor could not hide his desperation tone. "X-ray shots did not reveal the problem. Meanwhile, the kids were more and more intoxicated. None of us had seen sealed intestines in cases of salmonella. Swollen, yes. But never sealed. That was the reason, that the kids did not respond to treatment." But she knew the reason. It was the revenge of the Incubus.

In the four days, Michael had been calling her. On the call that she finally took, she was clear to him about her feelings.

"I did it with you the first time out of curiosity. Hendrick was nothing exciting in his lovemaking so I wanted to find out the real thing. I liked you and this provoked more experiences. The following ones I did because I felt I had a good lay. Unforgettable, I have to admit. And I still long for those good hard lays I lived with you. But what has happened has made me reconsider. You understand. I lost my three babies by the nails I fashioned to scratch your back. That is what carried the salmonella. Please don't call me anymore."

"But, dear, we could make babies replace the ones you lost," said Michael. "Hendrick and I have the same build and looks. They would look as if from him. What do you say?" She was shocked at his unrealistic attitude.

Before answering, she got an insight into the purpose of Succubus using Michael as an instrument. The Succubus wanted to destroy him with her jealousy. Like any psychotic-jealous woman, Succubus would entice him to be unfair to then punish him. It would take more time. Incubus enticed her to destroy her life. The Old Lady warned her. Succubus would hurt him but first would get rid of her. The feminine rules work like that. The two spirits were working together. She couldn't bear more destruction. Finally, she discerned what was going on in her spiritual world.

"I don't think I can do that. Your spiritual life is squelching mine. I am dry inside and you want to dry me more. After some time I'll be arid within my soul. It's as if you came from the death to bring death. You only understand sex and more sex, all the time. I don't want to ever see you. Sorry. We had good times but it is over," said Andreina and hung up the phone. *I wonder what could be the next steps for the Incubus.*

===

Hendrick's worries had another direction. After taking notice of Michael's message, Hendrick asked a detective to intervene in the home phone and cellular Andreina. The PI recorded all the conversations from then on. When he heard all, he took the decision to confront her with the recordings and goodbye her. He waited for three more days. Meanwhile, he acted ignoring the situation and would bed her making her enjoy their sexual rituals as much as he could. On Thursday, he came home early and surprised her with the early arrival. He took her to bed having her in the passionate way that she enjoyed so much. When it was over, he talked to her about the recordings. It was then that she heard the voice of the Incubus.

"Here's my final stroke of revenge. You will not be able to parry it."

Hendrick started explaining to her how he learned about Michael and the work of the detective. He was very formal. She lowered her gaze.

"Forgive me, please, forgive me," said Andreina, "this was something which I could not control."

"I am sorry, Hon," said Hendrick, "I cannot continue our relations with the distrust I feel right now. I delayed this decision to be sure of my feelings. I even continued going to bed with you like nothing happened to see if I could feel the will for renewal. But the distrust comes back." He paused for the idea to sink into her mind. "This is goodbye. We may be friends but that is all. I will not look for you as a future wife when you could not be the past wife. I am really sorry. Good-bye. I'll go off while you pick up your things. A taxi will come to take you to the airport so you can fly to your parents' home. There's a one-way flight ticket on the credenza. Yes, go there and do some meditation to iron all the wrinkles of your life." Hendrick went out, got in his car, and left. She had to go. The house was his property before marrying her. She started packing and crying.

"Hey, bitch, who won now, say it?" said Incubus.

Tammuz
By Pedro J. Ramírez

Tammuz, the child, was named so because he was born on the 10th of July. This month is the month of the spirit of Tammuz, the spirit of destructions and calamities. His mother, Jocasta, felt that she had a calamity when she got pregnant from the young hunchback Petronni Horn, who seduced and raped her, by her claims. She never denounced him to the authorities, though. She admitted to herself that, strange as it was, she felt attracted to him. But when she saw her belly blowing, she felt like destroying everything around her. Her life was a real screw-up. As if challenging her indisposition, when the boy was born, he was beautiful, of delicate and graceful facial contours, and promised to grow with a powerful build, as demonstrated by his strong kicking and grasping. He could bring joy to any mother but her. He looked healthy, robust with the rubicund clean-cut face of an angel and he was attentive, with an inquisitive look, to those who grabbed him. It was as if he understood more than any other child. With Tammuz, the theory of a blank tabula in his brain could be deleted from the psychology books

The child was very special, like his month of birth. The month for us is simply July but for her—bearing on the legacy of her Jew parents—the birth date of the boy is the month of the spirit Tammuz. She knew about the month of spirit Tammuz and what the spirit yearned for. She knew each Jewish month and what each month stood for. Jocasta had learned from her mother that Tammuz was an evil spirit that would take any human carelessness to do evil to men. This had nothing to do with negligence in the human scope. This had to do with sinning knowingly. When a disgrace happened among relatives, she would invoke this as the spiritual strike of God and would explain with a quick dissertation on Tammuz.

"If you know you are sinning, disobeying God, you open the door to the spirit Tammuz to come against you. His acts are of the most extreme evils. These are the ones that will hurt you for your entire life. Nothing temporary. If we sinned we have to suffer what comes from Tammuz. Because I sinned, I am in solitude, and I hate solitude and have wrinkles like a raisin, and I have always cared for my skin and hate wrinkles. But then I adapted. When you adapt, Tammuz comes back and does a novel treat to keep you living in disgrace. Now I have chronic health affections of which the doctors cannot identify the cause. This cuts me all opportunities to marry a good man. I feel like committing suicide but don't have the courage."

Her mental obsession: *All my strength is for making Petronni's life a disgrace.* This was the constant mental harping of Jocasta. This had made her become obnoxious making a toxic environment for those relating to her.

So, Jocasta lived her despairs while the child grew showing a maturity ahead of his age. He was fond of studying and learning and talking with elders. Some elders, claiming to own special knowledge and gifts, theorized that his complicated birth granted him special virtues. They explained that when his mother was delivering him, she was in a trance and kept saying "Tammuz, Tammuz, Tammuz" as if invoking a spirit. They could understand the invocation and concluded that the boy would have gifts from the invocation. She, on the other hand, wanted the boy to be a disgrace to others as it was for her. But gradually, she came to realize that the child could become the weapon she needed to go against this depressing community and, mostly, Petronni. This realization made her protective and come to love the child with that strange love you hold for a useful object. In her case, the object is to do evil.

===

The disgraces were around the child since he was born. At the moment of delivery, the midwife, while cutting a piece of cloth to clean the mother, cut the small finger of her left hand. When she reacted to her accident, she moved the scissors away with an upward swing so fast that stabbed the right eye of the lady who was bringing hot water for cleaning. The reactions were so aberrant that they forgot the kerosene gas stove. It inflamed and started a fire in the kitchen. It was most fortunate that the "rapist" hunchback, curious about his to-be-borne son, put the fire off.

===

As the boy grew, new disgraceful events happened. There was no logical explanation for them but all happened when the child Tammuz was around. When he was three years old, he played in the backyard with his little friend Casper at the time Casper's mother called him to give him a slice of cake. She invited Tammuz and gave him a slice. Casper decided to compete eating his slice quicker and taking all of it in his mouth. His mother was already gone and did not see what he was doing. He was choking. Tammuz saw him gagging, turned his back to him, and started playing with his Tinkertoy. When he heard the steps of Casper's mother, he pretended to be talking to Casper, but with his back to him.

"You see, Casper, you have to insert this card into this groove, bending it. When you stick in these two other parts, you can fly the little Tinkertoy plane."

"Aaagh! Casper, what's with you," cried the mother. With her cry, Tammuz turned around.

Casper was dead. Tammuz cried too and went running to get Casper's father. He came over fast. When he saw the scene, he dropped flat. He had a heart stroke. Tammuz had a sly smile.

As he kept growing, the disgraceful events continued. He always gave the impression of not being related to the event but was in the scene. The only one who related the events to the child Tammuz was his mother. Nobody related his innocent look to the disgraces.

By the time the child Tammuz reached fourteen, his hormones pointed the way; he started getting interested in girls. It was easy for him to get their attention for he was handsome with athletic looks, dressed well, and had very good manners. His body looked ripe, like a man's. He behaved maturely for his age and had the shadow of a mustache. He was a good student and helped the girls with their assignments. The mothers of the young girls in the neighborhood saw him as the perfect match and did not take precautions when he courted them. With a free path to approach the girls, he skillfully took the virginity of a few for he was very wise on sexual matters. His mother celebrated this; she had taught him how to prevent getting them pregnant. She hated those pretentious girls of the community who his son dishonored. They were so nose-up. They were in the second standing of hatred, Petronni Horn had the first standing. She had been making plans and waiting for what she called the "Day of Petronni." Pity! Take his hunchback off and he had perfect looks. He knew it. She had told him when they were younger. Telling him spurred his interest in having her. He was a cultivated reader, easy with words that flattered her and he was a rich inheritor of parents that had a catastrophic accident. He was a Notre Dame case but without the inferiority complex. When she realized what she had prompted in him, he was on top of her, in porta, ready to go inside and willing to spill. With her soft pleasure-pain feelings and his intense pleasures, he spilled in a recipient that was hot and ready to cook. She didn't want him to say how it all came to happen. Better let it go by, then. The community would treat her like a whore. Better for her to be his victim. This he stood with grace and never revealed her luring or her moaning of pleasure when he was inside her. Nothing happened to him; being rich has privileges.

Jocasta took her time for she wanted to do a perfect "Day of Petronni."

===

Years passed and Tammuz reached seventeen. He was so ripe that he looked in full manhood. This made him "most interesting" to girls and, Oh yes, also to some adult women. Some of them were daring enough to invite him into their houses and get him into their beds. His mother decided then, in the same fashion as the sweet sixteen celebrations of girls, to start readying him to serve the spirit Tammuz. She started by learning about the events provoked or created by the spirit. And she taught him.

Tammuz the spirit would crisscross the webs of the lives of people to make them go against each other or force them into a relationship that would bring destruction to those related. Car accidents were a daily chore for the spirit as well as family feuds and in-house accidents. All these and more with terminal or incapacitating results. These were important lessons to pass on to her son. But among these lessons, she was most interested in crisscrossing the lives of people. With this lesson, she would get her revenge on Petronni Horn now that he was courting one of those nose-up ladies, Isabelle. She was born six years before Tammuz the child. She was his babysitter when she was twelve. She professed great admiration for the child.

"Oh, my. He is so intelligent. He learns so fast. Oh, and he is so adorable. Any girl would die kissing him. I love him, Jocasta," said Isabelle. All this she said frequently celebrating the child with many kisses. Obviously, she had a crush on the kid. Jocasta had expected this to be the way to get to her and her family's wealth. But Petronni got in the way and was of the right social status for her family. His easy words and smooth style touched the heart of the girl and her family. Expecting the girl to feel for Tammuz was far off because Jocasta had a lower social level. These circumstances made for a better revenge now that Tammuz had grown to be a young man. Jocasta then instructed her son to court Margot, her younger sister. With this, they would stay close to the family. She decided that it was time to start the consecration of the man to add to him the ways and powers of the spirit.

"My son, you have to learn what I tell you. Observe the people and pay attention to what they talk. This is how you can learn what is of most interest to them and what it is that will make them suffer the most. That on which they place high stakes will make them vulnerable."

"What for, Mother?" asked Tammuz.

"To control them to your wishes, hear me with the utmost attention. Now, follow this," with the tone of a teacher. "When you find on what they place their high stakes, like objects, people, or whatever, you have to think either to take it from them, destroy it, manipulate it, or be the one who enhances it. This will require some thinking and observation. You have to learn how the person reacts and feels about those things."

"Oh, I see. I have noticed that Margot is very concerned with her virginity and Isabelle's. She says that this is what holds their respectability in our community," said Tammuz. "But I would like to marry Margot when we reach twenty-one. At twenty I will graduate as a chemist and I will easily get a job. I love her."

"Nonsense. You have already fucked enough girls and women in town to be concerned now about falling in love to marry. Keep on screwing them and don't think about getting married."

"But Margot is so different from the other girls in town," said Tammuz, "I like to share time with her, conversing on many subjects. She has witty remarks and intelligent opinions about various subjects. She has a good sense of humor even in the days of the feminine curse. She gives me value. I think that she will be a special experience when we get intimate." Tammuz had a good benchmark for he had many sexual experiences with the girls in town. His words confessed feelings for her. But his mother had other thoughts.

"Good for you. By this time she had heard that you had been in bed with various women and with many of the girls who yielded their pussies to you, virgin or not. Then, if in spite of knowing that, she celebrates your company, you can sense that she is after having sex with you. Her virginity is important to her, then seduce and lay or rape her. That will be for her shame. This is a simple situation. Start thinking of what you need to do to seduce her. You have done it to other girls. Stop being so poetic about a future sexual experience with her." Jocasta kept making the preparations to initiate him. "It is the time to consecrate you with Tammuz, the spirit," said Jocasta. "It is your birthday, day, and hour. Follow me." They entered a small room that she kept locked all the time. It was gloomy, with candles, camphor, and other strange smells, hanging herbs, and little pots filled with colored scents and herbs and leaves. It was almost dark, only the candles lighted the place. When breathing you felt a rarefied and dense air. It made you feel like going into another dimension, walking into a supernatural immanence that wrapped the soul.

"Get naked and stand in the circle on the floor," ordered Jocasta. Tammuz felt shy and embarrassed but obeyed conditioned to the authority of his mother. She started pouring oils and scents over his head and then rubbing them all over his body. He felt the embarrassment of his mother going into all his crevices and exploring all the hidden and intimate portions of his body. While doing the anointing, she murmured a prayer with the tones of an incantation. Suddenly Tammuz felt a hot wave flowing through him as if he were flaming yet he was not sweating. Then a cold wave. A feeling of power permeated his emotions. He could not understand it but it produced pleasure in him. Now he was superior. The feelings of love for others were gone from his heart.

"Tammuz the spirit and you are one, my son. You can do all the condemnation that you wish by just saying it. Use your words wisely to glorify the spirit of destruction and desolation," said Jocasta. "Remember to use your best words for revenge and death."

===

Three days before Jocasta consecrated Tammuz, Petronni Horn reunited with his cousin Andrej who had come into town from Africa. He had been for over ten years in Chad, Central Africa. He was a practicing Christian, a very devoted, man of daily prayers and keeping a sustained relationship with Yahweh, the Christian God. He stayed in Chad evangelizing the animistic tribesmen there. He had visions of things to come, which got realized shortly after. Petronni and him were very close and fond of each other. They grew together. Now that he was back, they met and spent hours sharing anecdotes of the times of youth and infancy and of profound themes on the supernatural. With the experiences in Chad, Andrej picked on the subject of Tammuz, the spirit of Chad.

"This is the month of Tammuz. During this month", said Andrej, "Chad will experience the worst changes in weather, and a higher number of crimes: robberies, rapes, assassinations, domestic violence, accidents, and corruption in government. It is a month in which there is no law-abiding, respect for life or property. Tammuz operates with the purpose to destroy the individual and sacrifice the community. It is a month of spilling blood and destroying, property and people. I needed a rest of this. Ten years was already burdening me; I need a rest. I had to get out of Chad. I, along with a few more, were the only ones fighting this spiritual force. We were fine fighters, but this situation renewed every year. The same people who suffered it renewed it with new pacts. Unthinkable, don't you consider? Nevertheless, I will return. I'll finish work here in town and go back. Don't know when I go back, but I have to return."

"How do they renew it?" said Petronni.

"They make a ceremony of scents, candles, and herbs in perfume and potions. It is a smelly consecration. They do this at night, in a gloomy environment. When they do the singing and the incantations, Tammuz will manifest with waves of heat and cold. After they do this, the events will start. The people take the events of violence as sacrifices to appease the demands of Tammuz. They bear all the events with the expectation that Tammuz will be satisfied and there will be peace. The animists are the ones who most strongly hold on to this belief because the manifestations happen through natural acts. If they are not willing to get out of this cycle, I am not going to give away my life for it."

"I don't blame you, cousin. I presume that you learned a lot on how to deal with that spirit," said Petronni.

"I certainly did. I certainly did. With what I learned," said Andrej, "I can tell you that the influence of Tammuz is in this town. There are too many accidents happening. That man in the hardware that caught fire handling something which he had worked on for years. The fire department truck ramming inside the house where they were to put off a fire. The fashion designer cut off a nipple to the model when fitting on her body a new lingerie fabric. The midwife never untangled the baby from the umbilical cord and got strangled in front of her. And a few others. They all follow a pattern. Fire, fire, then flesh, flesh. All these happen with ten Hebrew days in between. Take a look at the dates and consider that the Hebrew day is from sunset to sunset. The Tammuz spirit is in town. This spirit must have somebody sponsoring it. I have an idea who could be the patron. I'll do the work here but once finished I don't expect new sponsors emerging. Then I can rest, maybe."

"This has not happened before," said Petronni. "We had never seen accidents so frequent in this town. This was indifferent to me and did not pay attention. You are bringing new light to these catastrophes. But who can tell the authorities that all this is happening because of spiritual reasons? If I were to do this, I would be taken as crazy."

"I understand. But this will increase by the time we approach the middle of the month of Tammuz. Wait and see. There's a lot of work to do. But I must first make a trip to the University and visit their security offices." Andrej walked out, without speaking and not saying goodbye. Petronni stayed with his mouth and eyes wide open. He had never been so discourteous. He observed Andrej walking to his place. He had a long step that seemed to hammer on the floor. His curly hair gave him a boyish look contrasted with his formal dress with boring colors and his show of character. It showed that he was a man who liked fitness. His body was strong, muscular, and moved with grace.

Days went by till the birthday of Jocasta's son. Fatalities kept on happening. More frequently. They happened with the pattern explained by Andrej, as Petronni could confirm on the news. Petronni got concerned and his worries led him to one thought: the birthday of his son.

===

After being consecrated by his mother, Tammuz looked different. He carried himself with an air of grandeur and the young man's grace that made him loved by the people was gone. When he joined a group, it would not continue a conversation and disbanded. Most of the time he was a lone figure in social meetings. Women, however, approached him and would look for his conversation. He courted Margot and became his fiancée. Everybody noticed that she was in love with him by the way that she stared at him when walking by his arm. Hers was a state of hypnotic seduction. She had a well-shaped body. Her hair embellished her; had blue eyes on an oval face of thick lips. She dressed with finesse and prudence and walked without the provoking cadence of Isabelle. Two more years passed and Jocasta decided to celebrate the birthday of Tammuz. This she would mix with his wedding with Margot. She suggested that it was a good time for Isabelle to marry Petronni.

"Both have had enough time sharing to know each other. Celebrating together, all the differences will be passed. If something needs to be forgiven, we'll follow the model of Christ. We have four months to get ready," said Jocasta. Her proposal was much celebrated by all the relatives and all clapped at the idea of a big celebration.

Andrej learned about Jocasta's proposal. He went to see his cousin to talk to him. It was in the night and Petronni was visiting his fiancée. So, he directed his steps to meet Petronni at Isabelle's home. The three houses were within walking distance of each other. There he found Tammuz, who was courting Margot.

"Good night," said Tammuz, "come in and sit." Andrej ignored the invitation and looked directly towards Petronni.

"Good night," said Petronni, "something to worry about that makes you come here in the night?"

"Yes. Of much concern to you," said Andrej looking at his eyes.

"By 'much concern' you mean what?" asked Petronni.

"Enough for you to come with me. I am sorry. My apologies to Lady Isabelle," said Andrej. His eyes were frowned and his forehead wrinkled, "but the matter is of most importance." Petronni apologized to Isabelle and walked out with his cousin. Once out of hearing distance, he explained his worry.

"A while ago I had a vision with Tammuz," said Andrej, "the groom of Margot. He had a grotesque mask and carried poison potions in his hands. He was emptying these potions into glasses of soft wine for you and Isabelle. While he was doing it, he was smiling and looking toward a lady who smiled at him with approval. This lady was Jocasta and she murmured to him 'The day of Petronni' is today. The poison is not to kill immediately. It will go through your bodies, paralyzing your internal organs. Being inert, these organs will die, rot, and your death will be of an apparent infection. You will become a walking putrefaction. Once this starts nobody can cure it. Now, one question for you. When will you think is the best opportunity for this?"

"In the marrying ceremony," said Petronni.

"Very logical. Don't you think? You will have a toast," said Andrej, "after the party you take off for the honeymoon to another country. The poison will do its effect in the other country and everybody will conclude that you got an illness in that country. All the suspicion about Tammuz will be eliminated because he drank and ate the same as you. He will work another opportunity with Margot's parents when at any time they announce a trip to another country."

"Was that in your vision, too?" asked Petronni.

"No. But I would expect that to happen. They are wealthy people. He is not."

"Why would he do all this?" asked Petronni.

"Because he is not Tammuz by name only. He has been consecrated. Now he is Tammuz by spirit. All that this spirit does is evil. He operates with destruction and death. I am sorry that he is your son but he is to destroy, including you, unless he is destroyed before."

"How do you know that he has been consecrated?" asked Petronni.

"He has been. I feel it in the spirit. I will pray that you learn it too. I will not insist to make you believe me. I'll let God show it to you."

"OK. OK. OK. Do whatever. I have gone along with what you told me. Now I'll go to my fiancée. I don't want to look discourteous."

"Good night, cousin. Be ready to learn from your dreams," said Andrej. The night had become darker and a warm gust blew from the north like in the book of Ezechiel. *The events of the vision will be accelerated.* Tammuz was aware that Andrej knew. *He will not wait.* Andrej decided to go after his cousin and warn him.

Petronni was already climbing the stairs to be with Isabelle. When he went into the living room, Tammuz had proposed a toast for the coming marriage and they were about to drink the cups. Petronni slapped the cups and spilled them.

"No toasts should be done before marriage. It's bad luck. Sorry for spilling the good wine. We should do this at the wedding ceremony. I'll buy another bottle."

Andrej stepped in. When he saw what has happened, smiled, looked at Tammuz, and said, "All the innocents have guardians. Shouldn't we thank God for that, don't you think?" The face of Tammuz showed confusion, his eyes widened, and his mouth twisted. *How could he know what I was to do? Killing the one I love proves my deep consecration to the spirit of Tammuz. I'll have to work on a new plan with Jocasta.*

"Goodbye to all of you. God will be your shield, cousin because you believed in him." *It will not be necessary to pray for a revelation for my cousin.*

===

Back at their home, Jocasta and her son were reviewing the incident of the cups of wine. "Oh, that god damned cousin. Mother, how is it that I cannot read his thoughts? Damn him. Oh, fuck. Damn him. I hate his guts. I would like to kill him. He should be wiped off the earth and sent to his heaven," said Tammuz, pounding on the table. "Though it was Petronni who spilled the wine, his cousin knew that. What can I do, Mother?"

"Kill him. But now is not the time. Let's wait and think of a plan that does not incriminate you. Remember that he is single. Probably he is longing to lay a woman. But by his interests and tastes, he is not for a common woman. The woman would have to be a good choice. I'll work on that. Isabelle has always liked men of good figure and he has that physical fitness that every woman likes and he looks like the super macho that a woman would like to have in bed. I bet that she has some wild dreams about him when she compares him with Petronni and considers his bent back. First step would be to gain his confidence. Invite him to dinner. I'll cook something from Central Africa. He was enough time there to get used to their food and should be missing something from there. Find out what he could like from there. Invite him on his last weekend in town."

"I know what he would like from there. During a conversation at Margot's home, he mentioned it. It was a name like 'ball' with goat meat with berries all cooked in a sauce of dried tomatoes and wine."

"I'll check it out and find out what it is," said Jocasta, "Take care of inviting him for dinner. We are not to try any poison. We don't want to become suspects for anything. You are not to venture anything. Leave it to me. I'll make the cousins get into a feud for Isabelle. She will be the excuse for it. Jealousy is a powerful force."

During that same week, Tammuz invited Andrej for dinner. It would be on the coming weekend. Jocasta instructed her son to invite Petronni, too, but to do so when Isabelle was present. If Petronni accepted the invitation, they would change the day and exclude Petronni.

"I expect Petronni to decline the invitation for Isabelle knows of the past relations that I had with him. If he does, don't insist. That's what I want to happen," said Jocasta. "I would rather have Andrej come alone."

The weekend arrived. Andrej got dressed in a burgundy jacket and mustard pants and a soft yellow turtle neck. The colors blend so well with him that he looked fashionable and original. When he arrived at Jocasta's door, she was impressed. "Oh my, a man of God who does not dress black and white with a thin tie. My God. I hope Isabelle, Margot, or any other woman doesn't see you. You are a walking lure to any young woman. How did you come to wear such colors? They don't match but they make a total effect of good taste and novelty."

"Jocasta, why mention Isabelle and Margot among the other women? They are already engaged to marry soon. That's not right. And, by the way, the other guests apologized. They will not be able to come," said Andrej. *I asked them not to come* was in his thoughts. She smiled presuming that all was according to plans; not suspecting Andrej's intervention.

"You should see how Isabelle's eyes shine when you arrive. I can sense that she likes you over your cousin," said Jocasta.

"I accepted your invitation but we are not to get into the subject of women who would like me. OK?"

"I am sorry. Age grants me permission to say what as a young I would not say. I cooked boulé for dinner, goat meat in a sauce of dried tomatoes and wine, and got bread with raisins. The dessert will be dates in honey with roasted almonds. I understand that this a typical dish in Central Africa."

"Not typical, Jocasta. This dish is to gather the family under the spells of the spirit of Tammuz. A very powerful spirit. This month is the month of Tammuz. Only all the believers who adore Tammuz sit at the same table for dinner. They drink fruit juice mixed with alcoholic fruit drinks. All are in a natural state because they are animistic. I am so glad for your invitation. It makes me very happy, indeed. We can share a lot as you will see. In Africa, I used to sit with people celebrating Tammuz to explain to them the consequences, as I will explain to you." Jocasta's eyes were radiant. Obviously not understanding what he meant.

"You make me feel very happy, Andrej. This is unusual for me to receive compliments like this. I feel honored really. Much more because this is the month of my son. That's why his name is Tammuz."

"I know. You took a big decision when you baptized him Tammuz. Can we go to the table? Isn't Tammuz coming?"

"Oh, I'm sorry. He's coming. He's getting dressed. Oh, there he is."

"How are you doing?" said Andrej.

"I'm OK. Just hungry. Let's sit and eat. Mother, tell Danielle to serve, we are ready to eat, please. I presume Andrej is hungry, too." They all went to the table. It was a long rectangular table good for eight persons, two would head the table. It had no decoration. It was of flat taste like a silver platter of dull polish. Andrej took a head. Jocasta took the other. Danielle came to serve after Jocasta seated.

Everybody was very serious and didn't look tuned for humor. No spicy comments to relax the room environment. The ambient was ceremonious and filled with explosive vapors of tension. This contrasted with the silk curtains and the soft pink tablecloth printed with partying couples. Danielle finished serving and all was set to eat. Andrej started with his entrée, mushrooms with garlic and onion sauce. He ate with a monk's patience and tried to keep his conversation alive.

"Have you heard the death reports within our community?" Andrej asked both. "You should realize that the deaths for all kinds of reasons have increased ten times for the last week and keeps increasing. This is something expected in the month of Tammuz. This is a bad association with your name. Don't you think that it is unfortunate that you called him Tammuz, Jocasta?"

"I don't find this unfortunate," said Jocasta with a stern face.

"Do you like the name?" asked Andrej, looking at Tammuz to the eyes. "I presume that the name made you more interesting at the university aside from the novel intellectual achievements that you had there."

"The names add color to the lives of persons," said Tammuz, "besides establishing a purpose to live for. My mother and I understand very well the extent of the powers and the season manifestations of the spirit Tammuz. She studied the spirit before choosing my name. This is his month, his season for stronger manifestations. You can see that these deaths are of people who were careless and with a history of proneness to accidents and not related to my name, or me."

The dinner was eaten slowly and most of it was on the table. Danielle had come to clear the table twice to collect the dishes of the entrée but could not. Their conversation went on. Andrej and Tammuz almost had a duel by the way they looked at each other when talking. Jocasta, smiling, darted Andrej with her look when he started associating Tammuz with the local deaths. He smiled back.

"For common eyes," added Andrej, "what can be seen doesn't show much. What can be seen is not related to anybody. For common eyes, the deaths are normal events. For me, however, I can assert that spirit Tammuz is sponsored and this increases his power to provoke more fatal cases. The spirit feels patronized. He has a rep that supports his manifestations and renovates the spiritual power. Like it happens at the university that you attended. The death toll there increased five times when you started studying there. It was so much that you ended up alone. All the ones that died were somehow related to you. Your professor of ethics had some serious disagreements with you and choked when swallowing a boiled egg. He had his 'egg ceremony' every day. Two student associates were hit by a truck when running bikes on both sides of the road. If we estimate the probability of the truck hitting both, it is less than 0.001%. How about these two students that complained to your professor of Social Research in progress that you wanted to do a research assignment? But they didn't have much time for disagreeing. They died mysteriously. There are some more cases but they are not dramatic enough to mention. Would you say that you have a blood diploma? Loneliness is what comes out of these situations. Don't you feel alone?"

The face of Tammuz twisted with lips almost to snarl and with a dark look to Andrej, his fists closed, like ready to hit. *Why did Mother get into inviting him for dinner? This is worst than bearing him at Margot's home. Much worse.*

"No. I don't feel alone. I have Margot and I share with Petronni, my father, and even with you, and, of course, with my mother. As for the deaths that you mention, nobody could relate them to me. Thus I have a diploma, period. If they relate to a spirit, then who is going to prove it and how? There's no spiritual court in this town or country. There's none in the world I could say."

"You are wrong when you say that there is no spiritual court to settle these deaths and destruction. They are real crimes. Well, all this is beyond my intelligence. It is not my intelligence that brings these details. It is the intelligence of God that delivers me what I need to know. His spirit shows it in dreams, visions, coded messages, and symbols. Tammuz knows about this and, when his identity is at risk, he destroys all that endangers it, be it a person or object. I bet you that Danielle is overhearing. She should be told to go home." Andrej wanted to spare Danielle. On the way to the kitchen, to speak with Danielle, Jocasta noticed that she was effectively eavesdropping. She terminated Danielle and returned to the table.

"As I was saying, the spirit of Tammuz destroys all that endangers its identity. You are about to be destroyed."

"How come? We haven't done anything to destroy its identity," said Jocasta, "and my son has been consecrated."

"Right on, Mother. We have done the ceremony for consecration with all the details."

"Tammuz will not question that. But consecration has to do with a way of living besides the initiation. Family dinner is family dinner. All the participants have to be believers in this spirit. If there is a nonbeliever, the spirit considers this treason and sentences the believers to death. I have dressed in all opposition to him. The colors of the spirit are dark violet. My colors are in the opposite extreme of the spectrum, wine and yellow and I believe in Abraham's God, Yahweh. I am all the opposite of a Tammuz believer. You can draw your conclusion."

"Well, we are still alive, don't we?" asked Tammuz.

"For the spirit Tammuz death is a process. It will not execute a single terminal act. Sometimes it wants you to suffer the expectation and make you see how death approaches your life," said Andrej. "All the candles that you have in your secret room will start dimming till off. When they get off, your death process will start. Nothing will stop this process except your renunciation to the spirit of Tammuz NOW and acceptance to believe in Christ. It's your decision."

"I will not renounce to spirit Tammuz. Isn't that right, mother? We will not."

"We will not, my son. We will not. His is the power."

"But he will renounce to you," said Andrej. He continued with the dinner with no more reference to the previous conversation. He shifted to the dishes at hand. "The boulé is delicious. You cooked the goat meat? It is perfect. They blend very well while chewing and turn a tastier flavor that makes the cuisine excellent. I need to inform you that from this moment on you should not take steps to harm me. Just accept what I have told you and make a decision for life or death." He kept on eating and finished the portion served. "Do you use coffee or tea after dinner?"

"It shall be tea," said Jocasta.

"Be it tea, then," said Andrej. She went to the kitchen to boil the water.

"Tonight will be my night of prayers to spirit Tammuz to get rid of you in an accident," said Tammuz.

"I informed you not to take steps to harm me. Doing that will make spirit Tammuz act against you earlier. Repent and change your belief. Go and advise your mother not to pour that poison that she wants to use in the marriage ceremony into the tea that she is going to serve me. There is a promise from God to guard His believers against mortal poisons." Tammuz did not get up to advise his mother. She was coming with the carafe of boiled water.

"Did you pour that transparent poison that you are saving for the marriage ceremony in this water?" asked Andrej. Jocasta dropped her jaw and opened her eyes. The carafe slipped from her hands and crashed into pieces. "As you can see God protects me against such attempts."

"It could have taken six minutes for a man your size," said Tammuz with a defiant look.

"You will not see me die. I will walk out and… Jocasta, you will last till the day after tomorrow at ten o'clock in the morning. You will have the chance to see the candles dim. That will be your last sight. Then you, Tammuz, will fall. By that time I'll be in Chad."

Andrej got up smiled at them and left in confidence. His expression was relaxed as if nothing serious was being discussed.

===

Two days later, at ten o'clock in the morning, Tammuz saw Jocasta coming out of the consecration room and she exclaimed, "The candles are off." Then she reached for her chest, squeezed her left side, opened her mouth with a twist of pain, and fell in front of him. In a split time, he recalled what Andrej had told him after dinner. He beat his chest with the right fist, and cried, "Impossible!" His eyes opened in surprise and the surprise turned to madness with his lips forming a pronounced curl, and fell by the side of his mother's body.

===

At Chad, Andrej felt in his spirit that they had died. They would not have a chance to poison his cousin who was warned not to go to Isabelle's home until Wednesday. Jocasta and Tammuz had time to repent but refused to. Petronni would have the pain of the death of his son but he understood and realized that the wrath of the spirit Tammuz was in his destiny. Isabelle and Petronni married and went abroad for some time to put these events out of their minds. Margot was free and new solicitors approached her. Andrej wanted to be far from the events and from Isabelle. He would never return. He made up his mind and married Igoki, a beautiful black princess in Chad. Her blue eyes and firm shapes charmed him.

Yuri

By Pedro J. Ramírez

Standing in front of the gate of the residential mall at Westchester was a man of athletic build. He was dressed in military camouflage and had a hunter knife on the belt. He observed Pastor Chroom, who was on the second floor of his home. The curtains veiled the image of the pastor but his corpulence could not be missed. It was around two in the morning and the pastor was readying to go to bed—so it seemed—and dimmed the lights.

Yuri jumped the fence decisively and stood on the patio, expecting that watching dogs, human or four-legged, would confront the intruder. He felt the humidity of soft fog surrounding and hiding him and heard voices in the distance. The shadow on the second floor was still there. He had to take action now. He threw the rubber-coated hook getting hold of the steel veranda. Quickly started rapelling pulling his body. As he was climbing the wall, he had a strange sensation. He could feel chicken bumps of fear on his skin. He had never felt these in his missions in Iraq and Afghanistan as Navy Seal. But he was decided regardless of the consequences. Again, he stood still for seconds to observe if there was anyone to confront. Nobody. Then, he moved the glass door and the Venetian slides. The place had the touch of a plushy office. An ample mahogany desk, a table for pictures, and a big bookshelf, filled with books of uneven heights. The chairs were of straight lines design. Pastor Chroom had a heavy muscular body; he did not have flabby flesh. His was a powerful body and was on his knees, speaking softly, barely audible.

"I'll do it the same way I did with the Sultan bodyguard in Iraq. He was a man about the size of this."

"If the man coming in here today is prompted to and kills me, forgive, Father, his act. His act is due to his ignorance and lack of belief. But I beg you to make him believe tonight."

Yuri was amazed. *I never talked to anybody about what I am going to do yet this man knows that I am coming for him and that I am in here. He is talking to "Father" about me and he is without protection. "Father" must be that person that my sister mentioned asking for my protection in the missions.*

"Chroom, I am in here to kill you."

"I know, son."

"My name is Yuri. I am the brother of Yurina."

"I remember her. She spoke to me about you and your combat skills. She is a source of many sorrows to us in the church. A very pitiful case."

"To you, she is a source of many sorrows. But she makes me a living sorrow. You don't understand how I, her brother, feel for what you did and what happened to her. My grief is so much that I have forever lost the joy of living."

"The same happened to my daughter and I miss her very much. There is a word to name the child who loses the parents, 'orphan.' But there is no word for the parent who loses the child. Perhaps I miss my daughter more than you miss your sister."

Chroom was now suddenly surrounded by a tingling light. It was red with intermittent glows of brilliant silver. Yuri assumed Chroom had activated some kind of alarm. Yuri approached Chroom, knife in hand with an attacker's grip for a powerful killing strike. But Yuri felt a potent grip on his wrist that pulled him back, away from the Pastor. He felt foolish and powerless, like a weak child.

What the hell? How come? This man has not moved a finger.

Yuri tried again with the same pullback.

"My son, the Holy Spirit is shielding me from your attack. If you try it again, you will be on the floor. After that, don't try it anymore because it will be your life."

"What kind of sorcerer are you? Did you use this magic on my sister? How do you know that I will be on the floor on my third trial? How do you know it will be my life if I try it a fourth time?"

"No. The Holy Spirit has his own will. I only beg of him and pray to Him for your life. And I know, because He tells me. Don't act foolishly."

"I have killed many men and I haven't had any problems. My training readied me to do so. What is this that you call me foolish for?"

"Nobody can go against the spirit of God. Whoever does so is bound to lose no matter how powerful may be. God is Almighty. He is being merciful to you."

"Is He showing mercy on you? You lied to my sister. You preached her to lean on God because God would heal her cancer. She, who was so beautiful and attractive, died rotten and totally disfigured, with her flesh putrid and falling off. She leaned on God. Great thing! I have never believed in God... Yurina did, and see what happened to her—"

"Who held your hand and pulled you back? Twice it happened, didn't it? And if you try it once more, the same will happen."

Yuri tried a third time. Now, the grip was potent on both wrists and ankles, pulled back, and went flat to the floor. But he was not hammered against the floor. He was laid on it and pinned with extreme strength. He could not move though he had a powerful body and was ready for combat.

"I will kill you. I will kill you, bastard. I will kill you."

"You will not. God wants to use you. That's why He got you into here. His purposes are not easily understood by us humans. You admired the beauty of your sister so much… this is really the flame of the love you feel for her. But you saw how beauty decays. You love and hate because of beauty. But look around you, when people age, where's beauty, where is grace, and where's attractiveness? Why did you abandon the woman you promised to love when you were stationed in Iraq, the one living in the city of Al-Amaran? God will teach you a lot. Think and think deeply."

"What am I going to think about? Aghhhh! What is happening to me? I have turmoil in my mind with many voices. How did you know of the woman of Al-Amaran?"

"Shut up and hear the voice of God. Renounce to your thinking and you will hear the voice of God."

"This pain …! Oh, it's too much. I cannot bear it. What are you doing to me? I am so weak. Aghhhh!"

"Renounce your thinking."

"OK. OK. OK. I can hear a strange voice within me." When Yuri poised for surrender, the tingling light became blinding brilliant. He felt as if new ideas were being printed in his brain. His life and experience burst into his memories in a quick parade that he could not control. The image of Layla Arina, his lover, came to his mind. First with her beautiful splendor. Then as the victim of nuclear radiation, disfigured with bloated yellow eyes that spilled stinking pus and her reeking, pierced skin, blood stains on her whiteness. Suddenly, he started talking loud an incredible language that he did not understand and felt overtaken, powerless. Then fainted.

===

Back at home, Yuri took a long deep rest. When he went for a shave, he saw in the mirror that his hair was in shades of gray. No more of the youthful shiny black. He picked the card that Yurina had given him with the hours of the church and felt that he had to go there. He felt peace. A new peace.

Sadiel
By Pedro J. Ramírez

There are these teens who wanted to mingle their hands but felt shy about it. They walked along the east border of Lake Yosemite bruising their hands every few steps. She felt anxious to hold his hand but her feminine taboos would not let her. *Women don't take such initiatives. He should be aggressive enough to grasp and hold my hand.*

Sadiel was a man-looking teen but his age did not grant him the key to open the door to walk into adventures with the opposite sex. At sixteen years, he was handsome and attractive in all aspects. Black hair, piercing eyes rounded by long eyelashes, and bulky eyebrows that gave him a mature look confirmed with an emerging mustache. Bright, witty, and admired for his athletic prowess, he was also a social asset in the teen gatherings for his ability to play various musical instruments. He had not an impressive height, but other physical attributes over-compensated lacking an inch or two. He had still the candor look of a virgin kid.

Jossie was blond with green eyes. Her hair was curly and she combed it to let it fall in front of her, covering her breasts. Her figure was pleasant and well-shaped with the hips going into womanhood. Small shoulders. Rounded rear. The expression in her eyes showed knowledge beyond her age and bittering worries fighting within. She posed as being experienced but she was as virgin as him.

Walking by the lake made them feel belonging to each other. And the lake helped it. The breeze coming from it was soft and warm, the surface of the lake water was of soft waves. A few loose petals of flowers and dry branches floated. The shadow of the trees invited to relax and want solitude.

Sadiel liked to be with Jossie; he liked to be with her by the lake but his mother opposed it. Frequently, he questioned his mother producing arguments that always ended the same. While walking by the lake, he was mentally reviewing the scenes of dialog.

"Mom, why you don't let me go with her by the lake? What is going to happen?" Sadiel frequently asked. His mother's reply was full of wisdom that he was not ready to understand.

"Too many things can happen. If you want to know each other more, you can sit on the balcony here at home and talk as much as you want. Why go to the lake? You don't need to be away from your family. If you go to the lake, Adelita has to go with you."

"But my sister is too young. She's a nuisance," said Sadiel.

"You go along my conditions or you have to limit yourself to meet Jossie at the band essays."

"But, Mom, please."

"Don't you think that she should try to make a relationship with the rest of the family? Going by the lake it's only you."

"But I want to be alone with her," said Sadiel. "We want to talk and share so much."

"What for? Tell me. I know what can happen." He sensed what could happen, too. "And I don't like the girl and her attitude. She's a dramatic manipulator. Every time that I look at her, she turns her face." Mother Annete looked into his eyes piercing into his emotions. "I offered to give her a lift to her home when I saw her walking from school and she rejected it. Remember when you offered to take her home after a band essay? It made sense; it was twelve midnight. She mounted a drama slapping her face and crying hysterically. Don't you see that she wants to create division among us? I had done no wrong to her. What's in her mind? Have you asked her?" asked Mom Annete. She had the insight that the girl was under some supernatural influence and wanted to lure Adriel into her world. But had no evidence of it, natural or supernatural.

Sadiel always suspected that Mother Annete was guided by the Holy Ghost and wanted to protect him.

===

Jossie and Sadiel started sharing their thoughts and feelings with the band. He was thunderstruck at first sight. In her, it was a deliberate step to know more about him and she lured it as a colorful flower attracting the insect to be trapped. A soft smile, looking in his direction, eye meeting eye. Another smile. A persistent look. Those were the right colorful actions to trap him. Very soon a mild conversation on their personal interests closed the gap placing the insect into the nest of the flower.

While sharing at the band meetings and essays both started filling their emotional voids. This happened instinctively because they didn't have the experience to realize so.

When she was a child, her parents decided to 'serve the country' by going to Afghanistan. She resented this deeply. Her grandparents raised her. When her parents returned, she refused to go back to her parents. Why would she? Her parents had rejected her when she was a child. Now she can reject them. Now in the peak of her adolescent emotions, the need for parenthood is entrenched in her. Her emotional web was misconstrued. The grannies did not intervene to prevent the expansion of those voids and correct the web. Now she has the wrong build-up in her personality. She didn't have a role model. She reasoned that those voids needed the attention of a male, a male wise to guide and set direction. Tom, the brother of Sadiel was a good alternative. The brothers were so balanced. But her attempts to gain the attention of Tom were unsuccessful. Sadiel was the alternative. It was to her advantage that he was in her band. In her spirit, she felt that she had to be successful in ripping Sadiel from the fabric of his mother. Jossie fantasized about the idea of getting him away from his mother by luring him with carnalities.

"We should plan an escapade to be alone with more intimacy. Then we can decide what to do and be more natural to each other," proposed Jossie. She was not totally free to talk about what she had deep in her mind that produced so many waves of heat and swells in her body. But she had gained the insight to make the right insinuations to provoke waves of heat and swells in boys.

Understanding her proposition, he replied, "I would love to. Nobody could take the experience from us. Once it happens, it is ours to keep. I would keep it in me for the rest of my life but this is too risky. We are just teens. We should stop thinking about that. My mother is a believer in Christian morals. You and I are under Christian morals."

"You are right. We should stop thinking about this. But it keeps coming into my mind and I have a hard time fighting it," said Jossie. "Intimacies can be very dangerous. They can ruin our lives." But she was ardent for them.

Sadiel wanted to demonstrate independence by being the support of another. He could show that he did not need the motherhood cares of his family. Jossie would satisfy his spirit by having him become the man filling her voids. Doing this, he would display maturity demonstrating independence.

"I feel that I should protect you. I love to be alone with you and I don't want to be disturbed by the presence of others. I being the only one in the scene makes me your only shield," said Sadiel. "It is inside my spirit and pleases my ego. I don't understand it but the feeling is very special and satisfying. It has to be with you."

"What kind of knowledge do you have that can explain what you just explained? Are those words from you or from something you read or heard?" asked Jossie feeling curious about what he just said.

"I didn't read nor heard those words. They come out of my mouth without me reasoning them. After I talk to them, I reason with them and find the words very truthful. What do you think?" asked Sadiel.

"You are very right," said Jossie

But "words" remained "words." No action was taken to follow the words. At home, his mother reinforced the "inaction." When Sadiel returned from the band essays, Jossie's influence was fresh and the insistence of Sadiel had all its force to argue with his mother. But his mother prevailed with her arguments and, when necessary, by imposing authority.

When Sadiel and Jossie were in the school band, they had the opportunity of exclusive sharing. Nobody paid attention to what they did. So they acted more expressively to each other.

At one instance, he was sitting on her lap when Holly walked into the band room.

"Why are you sitting on her lap?" asked Holly.

"Because he is my boyfriend," answered Jossie with defiance in her look.

"Oh, oh. News for all," said Holly. Sadiel reddened in embarrassment, waited a few seconds, and got off her lap. Holly was a very beautiful Jamaican girl. She had green eyes and the shapes of a black goddess. She liked Sadiel and had made friends with his mother. His mother considered her a very correct teen. Sadiel knew that she would carry the news to his mother. And she did.

The rest of the group didn't pay much attention to what they did in the essay room, but fed rumors—adding more than what really happened. Fortunately, the news never got to the ears of Mr. Larsen, the director of the band and teacher of the music course. Mr. Larsen was particularly fond of Sadiel for he was very good at following the compass of the band and was instrumental in teaching the other students. Sadiel reciprocated Larsen's feelings with great admiration and respect. In a short time, there was a strong bond between them which everybody took as good and was never tarnished by accusations of biased preference. Sadiel's talent justified Mr. Larsen's preference. Within the context of this relationship between them, Sadiel was always cautious and scared that Larsen would confront him about his relations with Jossie. That made

Sadiel prudent when he was with her in the essay room. But the matter entered Sadiel's home.

When Sadiel's father learned about this situation, he had a closed-door conversation with him.

"What am I hearing, son? Why are you conflicting your classes with your interest in Jossie? You'd better be aware that as a man you can be so easily accused by a lady if you are alone with her. You could get serious problems; you are both ripe for sex. Now consider this: You go with this girl along the lake and there are solitary areas. Suddenly she starts crying, tears her blouse, exposes a breast, and accuses you of trying to rape her, what do you think will happen?" confronted McKane, his father.

"She would not do that," replied Sadiel.

"How can you be sure? Don't you remember that she tried a relationship with your brother? When he declined her relationship, she's now trying to relate with you. Why she insists on a relationship with our family? There are other teens your age that she can relate to. Why us? Could there be some spiritual reason? What do you think?" asked McKane, prompting Sadiel to think deeper.

"I never considered that," said Sadiel.

"You should be alert as a Christian person. The spiritual world will always try to squelch your light. Your age is perfect to do that. The deformities created in your spirit now will be most permanent in your life. You will have tragedy after tragedy in your course of life. Let God guide you. Meanwhile, follow the advice of your mother. She means good for you."

"But, Dad. I like to talk to Jossie. We hold interesting conversations," said Sadiel, his hormones prevailing.

"If it is an interesting conversation, you can hold it on the balcony, here at home. I don't think that we need to talk any more about this," said the father.

===

Mother Annete was deep into the faith of Christianity. She was a woman of faithful praying. During her prayers and sleeping she had meaningful visions that on time were realized. With this particular treat, she prayed expecting a message-vision about Sadiel's situation. After a few months of praying she got a revelation of what was spiritually evolving in the lives of the teenagers. She never expected the matter to be of those serious consequences. It was to impact the whole family. She had the vision of a skeleton with flesh only in the hands and the feet and a hairy black amoeba engulfing Sadiel and growing tentacles that extended to her husband, McKane, and her older son, Tom. Her daughter and herself were not searched by the tentacles.

With the vision, Annete heard a soft voice that told her, "Ask Jossie what happened to a teen at the school that she attended before coming to your neighborhood." Understanding that she would not talk freely to her, Annete commissioned Sadiel.

"Sadiel, I need you to ask Jossie what happened to a friend of hers at the school that she attended before coming to your school." Sadiel's eyes opened wide.

"Mother, what have you found out? Have you been making investigations?"

"Not me. But the Holy Spirit. Insist on getting an answer from her. I can presume that this is more serious than what we figure."

"But how do I do it?" asked Sadiel.

"Don't you presume to be old enough to be independent? You can start with this. Figure it out," said the mother.

"OK. OK. I'll figure it out."

Annete realized that she would have to pray more and fast. She disliked fasting, but for her kids, she would do it. She would do it at Bertha's home. Her neighbor, Bertha, was always willing to get into these acts of faith and spiritual warring. Next morning, she knocked on Bertha's door.

"Bertha, how are you? I had come with a special request for help."

"It is about your kids, isn't it?" Annete assented with a nod. "You can count on me." They sat in front of each and started praying. Soon Bertha had a vision.

"How much you commune with the teen girl that comes looking for your younger son."

"I don't like her defiant attitude. I sense some disorder in her life, something dangerous. I feel a spiritual clash when she is around."

"Right to feel a clash. I had a vision of a shapeless terrifying creature engulfing human bodies," said Bertha. "Let's pray so that Yahweh takes action from there."

They both prayed intensely. In a moment both started talking in a different language, non-understandable for each but coming out desperate. After this started, a strong wind blew into the place stirring everything but not dislodging the objects in the room. Suddenly a soft wind twist surrounded them. The strange language came louder from each. When the flow of the soft wind stopped they lowered their arms and silenced. They felt exhausted.

After resting for a few minutes, Bertha cut the silence. "Yahweh will take control. We have to learn to rest on Him."

"Yes, Bertha. We have to trust Him."

===

During a spring afternoon, the teens decided to take a walk, holding hands by the lake. The sun was setting but was still clear for going around. This was an opportunity that Jossie and Sadiel would not miss. They had skipped school to be on their own. Annete was driving to pick up Tom at his part-time job and to pick up Adelita at school. Being Tom a young man of chronic time delays he would hold Mother Annete back. The teens were elated at this opportunity which they had desired for so long.

When they got close to a bend (where they were not noticed from the entrance to the lake), Jossie rushed herself onto Sadiel and kissed him with intensity. He was shocked but reacted and responded feverishly. He felt his whole body roaring and felt an urgent will to do more. His system—not his mind—was in control after a powerful erection. She unbuttoned her blouse and lowered her bra. His eyes widened in disbelief and his body ached with desire. He was lost in his mind on what to do next. She pulled him to her and kissed him again. This time playing with her tongue in his mouth. And used her hands to caress and touch his intimacy. This made him feel an exasperating heat with an uncontrollable wish to be man into her. Then he heard a scraping noise on his right side. He turned his head to look and there was a blob noise on his left side. Then at his right, he saw a bronze snake displaying the fangs. To his left, he saw a jelly creature, black and hairy, widening a swallowing cavity. Both of them made him feel a deep fear. He looked at her. She was not seeing what he saw. She saw nothing. Only he saw it. He lost his erection and cried, "HELP ME!"

She released him and fled. He returned to his home with an ashen face. He wanted to get out and run but could not. His mother had not arrived. He went to his room and tears slid from his experience. He would not have to ask what happened to the friend of her at the school that she attended. When he analyzed and tried to understand what happened, one thought worried him: *Will the fear that I felt stay in me? Possibly yes but pray to God it does not. I risked the rest of my life for Jossie. Mother is right. Yahweh has an order for everything. I will not look for Jossie. Ever.*

Ivanno
By Pedro J. Ramírez

"I want to divorce you. 2018 will be the year to terminate our relationship. I don't want you anymore," said Merith.

"You don't have to be so dramatic. You sound like a first-grade school teacher explaining the same in so many ways. Your first sentence was enough to understand what you wanted," said Ivanno. He was undisturbed, with a poker face. She raised her eyebrows disturbed by his non-reaction "OK, as soon as I get the papers I'll sign them. Don't worry," he added and walked away into his room and went to bed. She remained at the dining table.

While at the dining table, she was into commotions of surprise and disbelief. She recalled how she lured him to make him fall for her. The technique never failed with any man that was of her interest. The technique of staring and smiling had been copied by her girlfriend Christy and she never failed. The technique was used for some days, then a cup of coffee or a drink, and the man was licking her hand. But it didn't work with Ivanno.

After a few weeks of using the staring technique, she approached Ivanno and invited him to a cup of coffee. It could be a drink if so he wished.

"They tell me your name is Ivanno. What do you do in these offices?"

"Why do you ask? What do you want from me? By the way, what is your name? I noticed that you keep staring and smiling at me in an embarrassing way."

"You should not be so discourteous to answer me with more questions. You could at least tell me your last name. I've overcome a few women taboos inviting you to sit in here."

"My name is Ivanno Santos. Are you satisfied? I have to go back to work. Excuse me", he arose, Merith rose her eyebrows and her jaw dropped. He went back to his office. He never turned to look back. *I presume that she is very intrigued. Being a blond she is probably expecting me to be subjected to her because I have dark skin and am a Latino.*

After her pass, the next morning, Merith stared at him without saying a word when he passed by her side. He kept distant and expressionless. He was cool as a marble column. Merith was to face the greatest challenge of her life. All this she learned when she could finally sit with him at the coffee shop. It was weeks after when he invited her for a cup of coffee. It was then that she learned that he had trained for the Sphinx style. He had studied to be a social worker and this pose was necessary when interviewing delinquents. When talking with her, he projected deep thinking and detailed observation. Those were academic phases of him that she was not interested in pursuing. She had in her mind enjoying the man. The less academic females could easily see an attractive man, elegant, classy looking. Thick, black hair. Always well and properly dressed. No tennis; shoes are always polished. This man was obviously for her and did not require much thinking. But some disappointments came on the way which prompted her to divorce.

After he got into his room, Ivanno, too, streamed into thinking about the past while in bed. He remembered that when he looked at Merith, he perceived a spoiled child always getting what she wanted. Most probably rich or high class, or of well-to-do parents. *I can see that she is well related to the social groups of her social circles. She has a good shape with an abundant bosom, blue eyes, wide hips, and round rear. I like all those accessories. From what I see when I pass by her, she is able to interact with people of all levels but prefers her social group and those at that level. She seems to be an elitist. An elitist without sophisticated ideas; a simple person of simple thoughts. She has a particular attractiveness that strikes away all the negative reasons I have. I cannot explain this in spite of my knowledge of human behavior. I feel her more in my balls than in my heart. Besides, it is a good triumph for my color to have a white wife. Much more if she is blond.*

He recalled what his mother used to tell him: "When you feel like that, it is because of evil spiritual reasons. Spirits are surrounding you to get you to act on what they want. Slowly these spirits will drain you of your good nature and destroy all that is good in you. Like the old saying goes: 'Grab them by the balls and the rest will follow.'"

But Ivanno could not bank his mother's thinking in his realms of rationality. *I'm too rational to be fooled by the spirits. I will have control of the situation. I will manage my life and rule my destiny.* But the balls can rule reasoning if the attraction is powerful. And it was.

===

At about 10 a.m., after disposing of Ivanno with the divorce proposal, Merith arose from the dining table and walked out of the house. Then, she grabbed her cellular and called her parents.

"Mom, are you and Dad going out?"

"No, we are not. We will stay home. We don't intend to do any touring. Your father does not feel well. How are you, dear? Come over and have a late breakfast with your old folks. How is Ivanno? Bring him over," said Morina. "But tell him to take a shower first."

"Ivanno is sleeping. He is for a long sleep and no shower. It's Saturday, you know."

"I know. I would do the same. You should be in bed with your husband. But since you are awake and out of bed," said Morina, "come to us. Don't waste time."

Merith had a good time with her parents with the caution of not mentioning a word about her coming divorce. After sharing time with them, she went to visit some girlfriends. They wanted to get together and agreed to meet at Merith's home. She called her home to see if Ivanno was still there. Their requisite was that they wanted to act freely in their party—no man should be there. She found that he was up.

"Ivanno, the girls and I want to have a get-together there. Do you mind moving out so that we can have the home for ourselves? We are about to get divorced and I want to socialize with my friends. Can you understand that? I want some freedom with them."

"I can understand that. Can you understand that I have some say in what you want to do? My answer is NO. Get your friends to move to one of their houses. They will not come to clean tomorrow the mess that they make spilling their drinks and crumbs. Ha!, last time one of them puked. And you never clean."

"But I promised them that we'd go home."

"Your promise, your problem. I didn't promise anything." Ivanno hung up.

Two hours later Merith was face to face confronting Ivanno.

"How could you do this to me? You are a real bastard. You have been always so antisocial. You are like a wolf. Do you realize that?"

"Ignorant. If I'm like a wolf I'm very social; they live in packs. Besides, do you understand what is the purpose of a divorce? It is to declare to the world that the couple has decided their lives will take individual routes. They are no longer in the same course. Yet you want to come and share with your friends at my home—a place you never cleansed before or after you make your special 'celebrations.' Now make sure you tell your girlfriends that you asked me for divorce. Now good night. I need to sleep. I'll work early tomorrow."

Merith was aghast. *He was always so cool and tolerant. So correct. And, in addition, he is going to work tomorrow. Tomorrow is Sunday. This has to be community service. What turned him into this new person?*

===

While Merith was out of the house, meeting her friends, Ivanno called his mother and informed her about the divorce. The other details about Merith partying with her girlfriends and spending her time with her social elite were details known by the mother. She had learned about these when she visited him.

Zorianne took the role of coach for her son.

"My son, I will share with you experiences and wisdom as the Holy Spirit guides me to tell you. For one, you have given away two essential things that make you a special person. You have given away your identity to conform to people who don't share your beliefs. And you have given away the time that you should dedicate to the things that Yahweh asks from you. You are not a man for a merry-go-round of drinking and partying without purpose. Share with believers. Work on community projects that will make you feel proud of what you do. You used to sing in the choral of the church. Do it again. I will be praying for you," said Zorianne.

"OK, Mom. I have been praying, too. This self-dump state I have has driven me into a deep depression. I have to confess that I was on the verge of suicide. I haven't bathed for weeks. Getting close to me is disgusting. I look like a bomb. I have been taken to court and held in the jail of the police station a couple of times. Merith sneers at me in despise. But I am enlightened on what I will do. The Holy Spirit will guide me every step. Good night, Mom."

"Good night, son."

Ivanno went to the bathroom and took a brush to shower. He brushed his skin three times to remove all the grime that he had. He cleansed himself as if he were to work in a surgical room. Then he perfumed his body with 212. When he finished his cleansing, he called his in-laws.

"Hello, how are you doing, Morina?"

"Ivanno, it is so good to hear you. Why don't you come over? We all can get together for dinner."

"No. I cannot do it. I am calling to invite you to Wallo's. I'm paying. We should meet there on Thursday at 7:30 PM. Is that day and time OK for you? Don't forget to tell John. Being retired I would presume that he would not have a problem with the date and time. Morina, I have to inform you that I took a "surgeon shower" as you say. You won't need to worry sitting close to me."

"Ha, ha, ha. OK. Be most pleased to see you. Now, wait a minute. I'll ask John. He's by my side," a brief interruption, then, "he says it is OK. He'll be most delighted to see you with your 'surgeon shower'," said Morina

"OK then. We'll meet there." *There are two days in between. I can clear any problem that may come up at the last minute.* His thinking was interrupted when Merith walked in. He turned to her.

"Merith, I invited your parents to meet with me for dinner at Wallo's. It will be on Thursday at 7:30 PM. You are invited. Get ready for the day."

"But I was going to go with Crissy for a show and she was going to stay here overnight."

"Then don't invite her. And I don't want her to come into this house. I don't want to even see her. Get that clear in your mind."

"But why?" asked Merith.

"I will not give you reasons. Just get clear that I don't want her to come into this house. You decide: show or dinner with your parents." He was not giving reasons for not admitting Crissy, but there was a special reason: Crissy tried to seduce him at a time that he separated from Merith. He felt so disgusted with her for being so unscrupulous that he did not want to see her.

Merith got mad but she was pleased with Wallo's invitation. It was a nice place and she felt secure with her parents in there.

===

The next morning Ivanno got up early, went to the bathroom to void himself, and took a hot shower. He dressed with business formality and walked out carrying his briefcase. She noticed the attire and opened her eyes pleased with the sight.

"You look splendid. Where are you going? And why the scent of 212?" asked Merith.

"To work. My work demands that I look professional and my presence should be liked. Goodbye." There was no reciprocity to her flirt. He was expressionless like he used to be. He provoked a shock in her. He was again of her liking but she had already talked 'divorce.' On the route to work in an Uber taxi, he stopped at the church and registered his name to participate in the choral essays at which he belonged a year ago. Then he went to a home of orphans to see what kind of help he could offer. Later at his office, he made a list from his cellular for twenty calls. He rekindled the relations that he had with people of faith. They were all praying for him but two of them really stunned him with their concern about his situation.

"Ivanno! It is really good to hear you. A few days ago I was praying and your name and image got into my prayers. While I was praying I had the vision that you were in a deep pit and hooks came out of heaven. These went over you and raised you out of the pit," said Roberto.

"Thank you, Roberto. We'll talk more about this experience next week when we meet. I need to make a few more calls," said Ivanno.

When he called a girlfriend, Altamira, he got a similar story but with deeper complications, "Ivanno, I have been praying for you. What prompted me was that I had a vision of you in a desperate situation. In this vision, you were struggling to come out of a pond of jelly mud. The more you tried, the deeper you went. You were naked and very dirty. Vipers were coming over you with their fangs ready to bite you on the head. From your head, you exuded pus and stinking worms came out of your eyes and ears. It was horrible. The Holy Spirit overtook me and I started praying loud in another language. A swift wind encircled me and I raised my voice and cried with a constant stream of tears. I trembled. Then a light came over you, raised you over the mud. White shining clothes and a shield came from a void in heaven and covered you. A flame burned the vipers that threatened to bite you. Then music and singing. When this was over I was exhausted. Now, are you OK?"

"I am OK. Better than ever. The love of God spared me and covered me for great purposes. We'll talk more about all this when we meet next week. Thank you for yielding yourself to the hands of the Holy Spirit. Thank you," said Ivanno.

It was to Ivanno's satisfaction that many friends have been praying for him. Some with deep feelings. He thanked Yahweh for these extensions of His love.

The prayers pointed to what his mother told him. His tears flowed abundantly over his cheeks and with deep emotion, he raised his voice.

"Thank you, God, for rescuing me. Now I will need your help to go on. Thank you."

Then he pulled his papers from the drawers and did his work.

Next day he rested. On evening, he took an Uber to go to Wallo's.

===

When he arrived at Wallo's, his in-laws were already there. John and Morina received him with an embrace.

"This is the Ivanno I knew. Always looking sharp. It is good to see you like that; you are recovered," said John.

"Oh, my. This is great. I love you, Ivanno," said Morina. And they conversed about some world affairs and the North Korean threats and the ridiculous statements of President Trump. Some entrées were served to wait for the main course.

"It's good to converse with you, Ivanno. You are always up to date in all these matters," said John.

"Have to. These are signs of times. And these subjects allow me to open conversation with the cases of social work," said Ivanno.

Merith walked in twenty-five minutes later.

"My dear, you have not learned to be on time. You should have walked in with your husband," said Morina.

"Yes; that's the way to do it. With your husband," said John.

"No; the way she's doing is the right way. She asked to divorce me. I guess that makes us separate persons," said Ivanno. "I can presume, Merith, that you have not told your parents that you asked to divorce me almost one week ago. You don't need to worry. I'm not going to make a scene. Meanwhile, we'll sleep in separate rooms if they don't take you back to their home. Now we can act very mature and have dinner. Merith, I didn't fit your specifications. Now I'll try to fit the specifications of the Lord," said Ivanno.

Ivanno noticed that his in-laws were staring at Merith as if she had come from outer space. They said nothing. Ivanno noticed a gesture of admiration and some gratitude from them for being prudent and staying cool. Morina broke the spell of the stare.

"She's not to come home. She had to take responsibility for her marriage and independence. She works, so she can rent an apartment and live by herself. Or get one of her girlfriends as a partner to pay the rent."

Ivanno continued, "We will stay in touch, John and Morina. You had been my in-laws but above all, you have been good people to me. I feel gratitude for that. As for Merith, I don't want to relate to her to avoid hurting her future life. That said, let's enjoy the dinner. The crab that they make here is excellent. They're spicy."

"I appreciate your honesty. We shall stay in contact. Make me your guest in your activities and in the choral. I think Morina feels the same. Don't you, Morina?" asked John.

"I do. You're divorcing Merith not us," replied Morina. Merith bent her head looking downward. She blushed with shame.

===

Two years and a half passed. Merith didn't adjust well to living in separate rooms. The times of his lovemaking lingered in her memories provoking swelling and fluids in her intimacies. She was reluctant to move from the apartment, holding the expectation that he would make love to her and satisfy her desires. He was well equipped and had the skills to satisfy; she liked it very much. After all, she thought, all men have a strong mentality for sex and yield to its demands. But his only relation to her was a demand to pay half the mortgage for the privilege of being in the house. Ivanno felt free of her nuisances and used his caring and lover's time to make studies and presentations to the community groups that he served. He tried music and composed several evangelical songs that became very popular with singers of the faith. In time he was well known in the community and the mayor of the city consulted him on social affairs to design better social assistance programs that could give good services to people at low income levels. His social life was totally changed from the merry-go-round of partying and drinking to social contributions. A few months after, the mayor made him a consultant to his cabinet to gain perspective on social problems. Ivanno had become an important person in the city. Merith regretted her intentions to divorce. With her divorce, she was giving up the lady status that she could have by his side.

Before the date of divorce in court, she proposed that he reconsider the separation.

"Ivanno, I think we should reconsider our divorce. Don't you think? I was so wrong in proposing it. Forgive me. Could you?" she asked.

"I can forgive you. That doesn't mean that I will not divorce. I forgive you for how you proposed it. You did not 'propose.' You imposed that you wanted to divorce. You saw me like a piece of shit. Now you want to ride on my new status. Sorry," replied Ivanno, "I have to go. I cannot keep on talking. I have to attend a meeting with the mayor and his cabinet. Tell your lawyer that he can read the papers, get the judge apprised of the situation, then I'll walk in and sign agreeing to divorce. We have nothing to split; this house is mine."

"That is really rushing. Why so?" asked Merith.

"Yes. This is all decided. Nothing new will happen," said Ivanno.

"I want to petition two things. Can I be a member of one of your community groups?" asked Merith, "and would you invite me to your choral?"

"Do whatever. I don't care what you do. In my mind you are dead. If you decide to move, this is up to you." He walked out. She started sobbing. He could hear her while he was going out. *Too late to regret your proposal. I am done with you, dear.*

The whoremother
By Pedro J. Ramírez

When Orlando was to climb the single step into home, his mother firmly grabbed his chin and kissed him fervently on the lips. He felt the wetness of her mouth. He was coming from his honeymoon. He felt embarrassed for his wife and got mad. Her kiss reminded him of inappropriate past experiences with her. More than inappropriate, these were sinful. Very sinful. It started a few nights after his mother had sex with his father. The night that they had sex, he had peeped them through the slots of the panes separating his mother's room from his brother's. He stood on the head of his brother's bed to watch. At the time, his brother was out drinking with his friends. Through the slots, he could see the rituals from the beginning to the orgasms. It seemed that his mother enjoyed it all very much. She would spread her legs wider when coming. All these images stayed in his mind for long. After peeping, he would masturbate with all these images in his mind.

The experiences started to happen, days after a peeping night, his mother had back pain and asked Orlando to rub it. She went to bed, leaned on her left side, and raised her robe. She had no panties so her butts were naked. He had seen them when peeping. This time they were at hand. They were thick and firm, round and beautiful. She was in a candid conversation.

"Your father is not coming to visit me this week. I'll miss him. I'll miss him very much," she said. Her tone conveyed longing. Orlando was not hearing much. He was very attentive to her beautiful butt, appreciating it with lust in his heart. Refusing to think about this, he kept on rubbing her back but felt the desire to rub her lower fleshy butts. His prostate contracted hinting an arousal and a desire to spill. His whole system roared with a sudden desire, and took a decision: pulled his dick out of his pants and laid it on her fleshy bottom. No doubt that she felt the warm piece of meat on her back cleavage. After about a minute, she grasped it and rolled to lay on her back. Looked at him and talked to him, with a firm order. "Pull down your pants and come between my legs." She spread her legs and he could see that it was swollen. She was ready. "I cannot stand holding it. Yours is big like your father's and I need it now." She grabbed Orlando by his waist with one hand. With the other, she grabbed his dick and placed it at the porta. "Go in. Go deep. All of it." While he was penetrating, she moaned and Orlando felt the spurt of her warm milk wetting his tip. The sensations were so awesome that he fainted laying on her. Her beautiful tits now were close to his lips. With renewed energies, he started a lip, tongue, and sucking work on them and she was ready for more. He then did some more in-out labor and had more moans from her. His prostate squeezed and an abundant spurt spilled from his pointer. When he pulled out, the mixture of their liquids overflowed on her ass. Then he decided to do something not thought of, turned her and did a soft penetration with the delight of her moans.

Similar experiences went on for a few years. Nobody suspected this sinful relationship. But it was disturbing him in the soul. It was a novelty for some time. He had the pleasant feeling of enjoying woman. Slowly he came to realize that this was not a "woman." This one was his mother. He started feeling tense and sensations of shame began to seep into his nerves. He became afraid that his sister would find out, or his father or his granny or his brother, or the neighborhood.

From those past experiences before marrying, holding such intimacies grew in him the desire to have woman. Then he looked for one that he would like and married her. He expected the relationship to be successful and get his mother out of the loop. He should not have any more sex with his mother. But she did not feel enthusiastic about him doing it with his wife and then excluding her. She had to be in the loop. At least once a week. When he confronted her, refusing to continue with the "malpractice", she showed him the visuals of all they did. Including her orals.

"If you reject me," she said with a threatening attitude, "I will put this on social media and claim that you forced me to do it. You'll be arrested. Most probably they'll kill you in prison. Some prisoners have very high moral standards. Your wife is pregnant with the little milk I left in you. Very fertile, ah! But that grants me the power to persuade."

He yielded to her demands. But this was creeping into him in an obnoxious way. Subtle escalations in his psyche, this was affecting his relations with his wife. When he intimated with his mother, he was feeling more pleasure with her than with his wife. He was afraid that the pleasures with his wife would eventually banish while the pleasures with his mother kept on increasing. This was not natural.

He was worried because that made him the sexual slave of his mother. No matter how much ashamed he was because of the situation, he decided to talk to Minga the medium of spirits of the neighborhood.

"Minga, I have a very serious problem. Years ago in my youthful lust, I dared to lay my mother. She welcomed it and a relationship started that I stopped for a few years. After I married she forced me to renew the sex sessions. I believe that she did this out of jealousy. She forced me with blackmail. She threatens to publish on social media some visuals that she recorded. Now it has become a problem in my spirit. I am feeling more pleasure with my mother than with my wife. I figure that she had done a spell for that. I need your help and your discretion. What can you do? What can I do?" asked Orlando. His facial expression was one of desperation.

"Let me see what spiritual forces are into this," she said and closed her eyes while tapping on her desk with a worn stick that used to belong to her grand-grandmother. She was invoking her spirits. "Show me, spirits. Show me the cause for the worries of this man who is in front of me," she paused, waited, and then revealed her vision, "I can see a shadow on you when you are near her. This shadow covers you and takes your thinking. Another shadow comes over her and does the same. A strange force makes these shadows merge intimately for sexual delights. It is a very powerful force joining Incubus and Succubus. She is not doing anything. These spirits act in their own interest. They have been instructed to do so." Minga paused thinking for a few minutes. "The alternatives are to kill her, move far away (with this you'll have to renounce all your achievements), the other is to divorce and continue with a sin that has the wrath of God. In time your family and all around you will know. You will become despicable to everybody and the law will put you in jail. There, somebody with gang moral standards will kill you. She will have the same destiny. Do you notice something when you are close to or in her?" asked the medium.

"I notice a transparent shadow on her. What can you do, then?" he asked to exhaust the last possibility.

"There is a lot I can do. But what I can do will make you suffer. It is not immediate death, of course. You have to consent and do what I tell you without deviations or shortcuts. Though it will happen in the spiritual world, there are laws that you and I have to abide by."

"I consent. No problem with that. Go ahead. My wife will deliver me a son. I have a son coming and I have to think about him. It is a boy as shown in the scanner."

"Very well. When is the weekday that your mother requires you to fuck her?" Orlando was shocked by her non-lady expression. "If this is tomorrow, undress. Don't get excited. This is not the first time I do this. The difference is that your case is more intense and demanding. In time, it will convey death."

"It is tomorrow. I will undress," he said and stripped.

"I will anoint you," she said. "While doing this I have to touch every part and hole of your body. Don't be shy about it. I will be doing it technically."

She lit some craft-made candles of perfume and she took some bottles of oils from the shelves behind her, poured them on his head, and let them slide on his body. Then, with her bare hands, she spread the oils on his body and in a low tone sang some chanting words. They came out like hissing whispers. Orlando could not decipher what they meant. When she arrived at his intimate parts, she sang a guttural chant, the voice raspy while grabbing them in her palm. Holding them, she poured oil from another bottle that had been put aside to use at this moment.

When finished, "Put on your clothes. Don't shower," then picked up another bottle of oil, "but anoint yourself with this oil before laying her. Don't worry about the smells. She will only feel the smell of this last oil which she will not remember the next day. Give her a good passionate lay. Make her feel good like nothing has happened. Celebrate the orgasms. Don't ask her anything after you both come. When you go back to your wife, shower very thoroughly before doing the work on her. Make sure that you shower before."

"OK. I will do as you say," said Orlando.

"Remember. It is important that you follow my instructions."

During the night, Orlando went to visit his mother. She was waiting for him by schedule. His performance was excellent. The copulas were intense and lasting, taking her into several orgasms. She was very pleased and confessed some of the sensations.

"My closures were intense and from deep inside. I felt like sucking you into myself. It was like never before."

Starting to dress, he announced his leave. "I got to go now. I have to buy some groceries tonight. Tomorrow I will not have time to shop. I'll be out of town solving a problem at a subsidiary of the company."

"OK. Go with God." He left quickly. Went to home. Showered brushing his body in detail, slept a while, and had his wife. His pleasures had higher levels but not as he expected.

===

The next day, in the morning, Orlando felt like a floating feather. He felt so relaxed that he approached his wife again before going to work. This time he felt intense pleasure as he expected to feel with a woman that he liked and desired. He concluded that the works of Minga were yielding good results. He expected that, as days and weeks passed, the pleasures with his wife would be more delightful. His work assignments kept him six weeks away from his house. He welcomed to be away from what he now considered his mother's molestations. The following week she asked the father of Orlando to come and be with her. She could not miss having a man. *"I yearn for you, my pleasure,"* she told him.

By the fifth week, his mother had an unbearable headache and felt a troubling itch between her legs with a thick stinky mucous thing coming out of her. The smell reeked terribly. She decided not to come out of the home. Investigating her cause of illness she called Orlando's father but he was scrupulously well and healthy. But she was unbearable to have around. She was so ashamed that called her son advising him not to come Wednesday until advised. She understood that her attractiveness was useless. She did not meet with her husband, or a lover that she had as backup. The malady kept on growing all over her body. She rot, everybody had to be distant from her. Within a year she died. By that time her grandson was born, a child of grace that she never saw.

High School Poet
By Pedro J. Ramírez

Milton was in constant reverie with the poems of García Lorca. This was his favorite poet. All the writings of Lorca were a great inspiration for him. Milton felt within that Lorca had his same spirit. In Lorca's poems, he could filter the unrest of his sexual urges for other men. Milton secretly admired this poet for his sincerity and his discretion while revealing his inner feelings for other men. Reading some news from Spain, he learned more about his feelings. His great love was a man. This man appreciated Lorca's love and reciprocated the poet. He wished that his close friend, who was so much macho would reciprocate him, too. It would be perfect. But he did not see in Milton the traits to bend for him. He was respectful and to the point. He was always relating to women, talking about them, making passes to them. He also shared some love moments that he had with these girls at the school. Imitating some of that, Milton presumed to love and want Nicolasa while he was in intermediate school. He was after her making all kinds of passes. Then, when he was in high school, he presumed to love Sarita. This was his peak. For Sarita, he wrote a poem that became a high school classic. But a recently arrived neoyorican conquered her love for Milton's aggravation. Milton felt shy with the girls. In his mind, he sensed that he would not be understood; he felt like a foreigner to them. When he looked himself at in the mirror, he was convinced of being a stranger to others. Most of his friends got girlfriends and he was alone, more isolated with the reveries of Lorca and with the knocks of realism forced by Benito.

The young and apparently innocent Benito harped and constantly reminded Milton of his upcoming sexual trends. It was open bullying. He did it very openly and Milton resisted it adamantly.

Benito's harping was constant. Milton responded fist fighting his school peer. The Coliseum for these encounters was an open lot close to the school. All the other kids celebrated the event. Neither of them would yield though Milton always had the worst part because Benito was a sturdy kid that grew up in a ward of daily fights and he was a good pugilist with the punch of a street fighter. Milton looked fragile compared to Benito. He did his bullying before and after the fights. None of the other kids, out of ignorance perhaps, bothered to look at Benito's expression: he had the conviction of a revelation.

"You are a homo. You make passes to Nicolasa to presume to be macho but she is not going to take you seriously. She sees you like what you are... a freaking homo. "This provoked Milton to go to him to strike a punch. During the fights, Benito would keep on calling him that and more. At the end of the fights, when their friends separated them, Benito would still yell to him "HOMO."

Milton came to feel relief on his high school years because Benisto had left with his family to live in the States. Milton now had relations that did not bully him. Other close friends, are William, Peter, and Marcos. But these withdrew from him slowly, for no obvious reason. The only one who kept a close relationship was Marcos. He was very close and Milton would share spiritual secrets with him. A well-kept secret was Milton's origin.

"Marcos, I will share with you a secret that was revealed to me and my parents by a medium of spirits while at a grand meeting. You are not to share this with anybody else. They revealed that I belong to a race out of this world. This is why my features are not common." Though surprised by Milton's confession, it led to meditation to explore the truth in the idea. Marcos did not argue. Just kept the idea to himself and searched in his mind: The idea seemed logical by what he had heard from his grandmother, the medium of spirits in his family. Besides, Marcos did not want to hurt the relations with Milton. He let it be. Milton also shared his writings with Marcos.

Milton's poems exposed his intimate feelings. He would frequently read these to Marcos. All of these talked about men sleeping naked by flowing waters while the current of water caressed their bodies in the intimate parts, arousing in the laying young character the will to intimate. While reading those poems, he was very emotional, with hard breathing. He would raise his head and look at Marcos with the lingers of emotional hopes of reciprocation. But Marcos took his expressive emotions as the sentimental state of a poet with inspiration. As time went by, he felt more attached to Marcos, his emotions rooting deeper into him. He thought constantly about him. In his dreams, Marcos, being strong and of a good fit, was the protagonist as a protector. These dreams made him happy.

Marcos made great company for him. He enjoyed being at home alone with Marcos. He was his source of emotions. There was not a normal source of affection at his home. His father went home at lunch without even saluting the visitor or kissing his wife. He would just walk in, have lunch, and get back to work. He gave the impression of holding a secret resentment for being emasculated. He did not make a model "man of the house" or the lover of the woman of the house. She did not inspire, either. She was a bore that gave the impression of pleasing the man by laying passively in a submission protocol to comply with being a wife. And she was ugly. Had all the looks and displayed a moralistic tune. He, however, was a handsome man but with the rictus of a man trapped against his will. He was the ceramic flower adorned with poison ivy, her.

Stemming from her low esteem, she projected dominance and a compulsion to control as evidenced by Milton's friends when celebrating his 18th birthday. Two of the girls who were student associates carried a small cake and a gift to his home. When they handed the gift to him, his mother grabbed it from his hands, unwrapped it, and examined it not minding the graceful visitors. Looked like she was appraising the gift. After her examination, she returned it to him as if in approval. The friends felt that Milton was a daisy that had to be protected. After a few more visits from these friends, one of them made a deep observation.

—With her emasculating character with the men of the house, his father probably has another woman. He is handsome and with appealing looks. She has a long horse face, with crooked teeth, the lips of a clam, and bursting eyes. His religion is holding the marriage, not love or even attraction. One of these days he will leave her. Poor Milton in the middle of all this. Being young and with his hormones erupting, he must already feel castrated.

Another friend added a profound confirming observation. —This is the wrong environment for a young man of Milton's talents. He is into arts. But his arts are sophisticated, not very man-like by traditional standards: Poetry. That creates a serious disadvantage for him. Besides, his friend is Marcos who is too advanced in relations with women for Milton to catch up. Something bad is going to happen—, pausing and then, adding as an afterthought:—I feel that he is isolated. Nobody with whom to share his feelings and thoughts, without a way out. Poor man. He must feel lonely.

A third girlfriend elaborated on his relations. —He is shy and had never been successful in luring a girl with his rapping. He does not even have good relations with the rest of the class; is like a hiding ostrich, always avoiding people. He related only with a few and has never expanded his relations to the rest around him. Now that we are going into university, I wonder how he will react to a new level of bullying and crudities.

His mannerisms and gestures made him obviously noticed by his peers. His distancing did not help to make relations and the co-students did not feel free to approach him. His life was of loneliness. He experienced affection with Marcos during his adolescence and that was the only model out of his family circle. At the university, he was too shy to relate to the young women and was afraid that the young men would bully him. He started to feel attraction for the young men instead of the young women. He had no model to feel the attraction of women. He noticed that he had strange sensations for men, as he felt for Marcos. With Nicolasa and Sarita all he had were failures; only with Marcos, he had reciprocated attention. Milton could not focus on his sexual attraction and those confusing thoughts crept into his mind. His poem in High School for Sarita was his last spurt of feeling for the opposite sex. He was not feeling again for girls; he was feeling for boys and it was pleasant. He yearned for a boy like Marcos.

His thoughts overtook his mind: *But this avenue is not approved by my father, mother, friends, or any relative. Not even by Marcos if I confessed that I had fallen for him. My heart and my body are his. But Marcos likes girls and many girls like him. He is not going to give up a girl for me. Which boy-boy would go over that? I am alone. Alone. Very lone. What is life if you do not have company to share it with? To share my thoughts and feelings like I used to share with Marcos. But now he is distant from me. Very busy with his girlfriend and university studies. Soon to marry. He will have a woman. I do not have the right organ for him to make love. And I know that he would prefer a girl, a woman. He knows the pleasures of having a woman. He confessed to me that he already experienced sleeping with two. He has become a man. I would like to have a man. I need to feel that he shares his soul with me with his penetration. I live loneliness. Loneliness is the real land of nowhere. The land of no purpose. The land without coexistence. The land of the dead. That is where I have to be. I will need to travel there.*

After a few weeks of isolation from his thoughts, Milton's mother talked to him. He confessed his feelings and the yearning for male company and the indisposition of female company. His mother talked to her husband, who had been alienated from the situation. He made his efforts to contact a woman for Milton. His reasoning was that if Milton had sex with a woman, he would be interested in "being a man." Milton learned about the intention of his father and felt so ashamed that Marcos could learn it, that he isolated into a cocoon of emotions. He would travel to and stay in his world: *loneliness.*

During a night, alone, Milton decided to travel to his world; loneliness, nobody else could be there. He readied for it. He went to his father's closet and picked up his cow skin belt. It had the perfect length for the trip. He circled his neck with it and circled the pipe of the bath curtain, stepped up on a chair, kicked it, and hung with a soft swing. The trip to his new world has started. It was fascinating.

He saw colored sparks. A peaceful silence. He closed his eyes to have these for himself. He was not to share that. Then the travel sped and he could not feel. He arrived. All was black. Milton died.

Wrong Incision
By Pedro J. Ramírez

He was ready for the ball. With this six feet with a good body build Dr. Mormon Kellly looked attractive. His tuxedo added elegance. When he walked in, women looked in his direction. He was a man of sex appeal. His professional performance added a spark of self-confidence to his sure steps. She was walking in, too. He was struck by her looks and the imposing swiftness in carrying her dress of open cuts on the sides and long breast cleavage. Her back was white silk with the black dress starting at her waist, close to the beginning of her bumpy rear. A strong want for her seized him when looking into her eyes. Her lips spread softly, like an invitation with a refrained whisper. The lust between them was like reminiscent bolts of high energy. Her lids lowered shyly when a man held her arm. The man was Armand Assante, a wealthy signore of high social circles. She was Morgana. He was her husband. Then she felt embarrassed with her lustful thoughts. Guessing her guilt, he looked to the chandeliers pretending not to be interested in her. Nobody noticed their mutually inclusive looks of so many secrets.

The orchestra continued with soft background music. Everybody kept on with their relaxed chatting. Armand's neck twisted to scan the room. She avoided looking to the sides. When he noticed her intense look, he was baffled. He felt disoriented. *A married woman. Oh, no. His thoughts were interrupted when an arm extended to touch him.* This was Doctor Cavening.

"Doctor Kelly, I need to talk to you. If you can allow me some time, this will be very brief. Could you come with me, please?"

Mormon followed him and the man stopped in front of a young couple. This was Armand Assante and his attractive wife. Mormon got tense and nervous.

"I will not go into the necessary details that you will be requested to take care of. They will share a delicate health matter with you," said Cavening.

It was Morgana the one who started the briefing. "My husband, doctor Kelly, has a spinal cord problem. Doctor Cavening has referred us to you for a consultation to diagnose and see if he will require neurosurgical intervention. The pain stiffens him and is afraid that he may not be able to walk."

"Can you take care of me? I'll make myself available any time you say," said Armand. "I would like this to be done soon. As soon as you can. Is it possible that you to postpone or cancel some of your patients and line me into an earlier queue? I'll pay you well."

"I don't have monetary concerns with my patients. And I can add, much less with you. You are a man of wealth," said Mormon. "The conditions of my patients are what guide my decision on you. But there is none that will demand special attention now and I can book you. Say you go to my office within two days for a thorough check-up. Then I'll need to separate a surgical room to intervene with you. The protocol for this intervention is very detailed and you have to be ready for it. We will resolve this in three days. Then, recovery for at least one month. No efforts during that time."

As agreed, all was set for surgery and Mormon was cutting Armand's spine after coming out of a party of hospital personnel. It was exciting and with heavy drinking. Now Dr. Kelly had the scalpel in his hand. He had already made an overall cut along the spinal cord to explore the cause of the pain of the patient. He was starting to sober from the party-drinking but his hand had a mild shake and his fingers did not have the sensibility to feedback to him if he was on the right path. He was approaching the white nervous center of the lumbar. Now he was Between T-12 and I-1. There he noticed a bone excess that was pressing the spine. It came shaded in the X-rays because it was hidden by the spine and some front organs. He could not depend on the camera display on the monitor to effectively handle the excess bone which was the cause of the pain. He was dependent on his now-unstable skill due to the alcohol. He was hesitant and he had already cut too much. He wanted to ensure an accurate cut but, due to his poor sensibility in the fingers, he pressured the scalpel too much and cut into the fiber of the nervous net of the lumbar. The patient will suffer serious consequences from his waist down. Mormon kept all to himself and played the cool cat not revealing a worried face or getting nervous. He realized that this could cost his career because the patient was a member of the social elite of London, as well as his wife, the luring Morgana.

===

After two and half months, Morgana went to Mormon's office. She had been undecided to do it because she sensed that he liked her and he was a very attractive man. She made sexual fantasies after hearing him talking at the party that both attended. She still recalled some of his deep phrases: *"Sex, desire, and love have to stay in the feelings like good sisters; always together. They are the sustainer of noble feelings and tragic acts. They make roots in your nervous system." "Love without the physical expression of sex is a concept for population attrition. Only governments sponsor it." "Politics is the highest expression of selfishness; all is for one and nothing for others." "Literature is good only when it flatters the intelligence of the reader." "History is something somebody else tells us. Events are the ones that rule the future."* She enjoyed his conversation and the sparks of his thoughts. Armand, her husband, came across as a man of trite thinking. Compared to Mormon, he was an article of boredom. This made her think of him during her nights. Thinking of him led to fantasies. It has happened so frequently that his presence gained familiarity in her life. It was like he lived with her. Her desire for him became powerful. Seeing him reminded her of Greek sculptures. Thinking of him, wrapped her into an act of lust and sexual fantasy that drained her energies. All this she kept to herself. The nurse-secretary interrupted her reverie.

"Ma'am, he's waiting; you may go in," said Rebecca.

"Thank you," Morgana replied and walked into the room. "Good morning." With decisiveness, she opened with the question she had in mind. "Dr. Kelly, what was it that my husband had? He was a sexually active man."

Perceptive of the undercurrent in her question, he replied. "Implicit in your question is that he was sexually active. How are you relating this to me?"

"The surgery. Did something irregular happened while doing the surgery?" None of that Mormon was to admit. He was not ready for that. Not now nor ever.

"I would rather ask if he had an accident that could be reflecting now. Or, does he have long-distance drives in one sitting? Or horse riding for long trips? Long meetings? Does he do long tracks of bicycling? Those are things that could be hurting him now. They tend to have hidden effects that show when you are older. We have to ask his parents or relatives about this"

"His parents died in a car accident and there are no other relatives to ask. Oh, my. This is a life cruelty to me. We used to be so compatible and always ready and willing. Oh, God. What am I going to do now? I'm going to miss much of him. This kills our sex life. I have a problem.

"I don't know what to tell you," said Dr. Kelly, trying to swallow with a dry throat the facts that he was hiding... "You will have to look for a new style of sexual relations."

"What other style? I am not related to 'styles.' "A good fuck for me is just that: a good fuck. To me, that means getting a rock-hard dick inside me and a spurt of warm spill deep inside. That, I love. Nothing replaces that. Too many days have gone by and I miss a deep penetration."

"Morgana, please stop. You stir my imagination. You are very attractive to me and raise wild thoughts and feelings. This is embarrassing to admit but when I see you I cannot help but get excited and—" said Dr. Kelly, swallowing hard. His eyes shrinking.

"And what?" she questioned with an emotional burst.

"—Already have a rock erection. Please leave. We can talk more later. You are too graphic in your descriptions."

Her facial expression changed and she got into a sudden rapt of wild emotions. There was an unequivocal look of lust in her eyes when staring at him. She approached him, pulled him by a hand, sat on the desk, and spread her legs. He felt the call and pulled his thing and thumped it into her with a strong thrust. She moaned and he groaned. Like jungle beasts. This was a very primitive experience for two highly educated homo sapiens. After exhaustion, they realized their imprudence and apologized to each other.

"My God. I don't understand how we have gone this far," she said while adjusting her panties and dress.

"Oh, Holly. I don't either. This is a realized desire but so wildly done. So little thought to do this. I am sorry. My God, there was so much pleasure. So much like never," he said. "Please go, now. I don't want this to happen again. If you stay I will want more."

"Me, too. I'll leave right now." Lowering her sight, "Sorry. Very sorry." Turning her head, "I have to confess that this is a realized desire, too. Bye."

She left. He was in a turmoil of confusion. She was into guilty pangs of adultery. *But, Oh, very satisfied in her yearning for sex and wanting more deep pleasures.*

===

Morgana decided to return to her home late pretending that she had some business meetings and other enterprising appointments. This gave her an unembarrassed expression if Armand was awake. She went directly to sleep, claiming to be tired. She didn't sleep well. Her mind went in all directions thinking about the affair that she had earlier. She felt "unclean" for having been an infidel, her rationality justified the experience with Mormon, being a woman lacking a man for long when she was used to having it, more than once, daily. At the same time, she felt that the intercourse with him was worthy because she experienced the deepest satisfaction of her life and wanted more. The solution had to be divorcing. In the morning she was going to ask Armand to free her. Fatigued with the mental gears working for so long and the relaxation of sexual pleasure, she slept. But Mormon could not hold his passionate thinking about her. His thrust thumping into her was so macho-satisfying that it kept running in his mind like a re-run movie of high pleasures. He wished he had recorded it. He wanted more of her. It was deeply satisfying. He had to have her again.

In the morning he went to his office. His friend the nurse Barbara was waiting for him. They had dated a couple of times and she wanted more of him. But after his experience with Morgana, he felt that he could not do a mating play with the nurse. To convince himself and get Morgana out of his wants, he decided to go out with Barbara and dated her after work hours. After four in the afternoon, he picked up the nurse at the hospital lobby and went to his apartment. She spend two nights with him and was very satisfied with his performance. But she could not get from him a single orgasm. He simulated that she was pleasing him and she was fooled by his faked orgasms. But he was not fooling her. It turned out to be frustrating for her that he didn't invite her to come the following week. She decided to be patient.

Morgana felt all kinds of twists in her body wanting the man that could produce in her such deep pleasures. She sensed her internal dimension as the perfect fit for Mormon. She waited for a few days to see if her spills and wetness would be overcome. This was to no avail. She started getting tense and gloomy. Several times she picked up the phone to call Mormon but decided not to. A week after her last temptation to call him, he phoned her.

"Morgana, I felt like apologizing for my imprudence in your last visit to my office. Please accept my excuses. How are you feeling?"

"Lousy. But hearing you makes me good. Same from my end. I need to apologize, too," she said. "I would like to visit your office for diagnosing Armand, but I am afraid to do it."

"You can come anytime you wish. Maybe this is a good way to try our self-control," he said.

"If you say so. I'll try it. We need to make sure to overcome this feeling. I'll go there in a few minutes. I am close to your office."

When she arrived at his office, the secretary, Rebecca, instructed her to go in directly. No need to wait. He had blocked two hours in the afternoon for her. When she saw him, her system got in high gear. She didn't even salute. She climbed onto his desk and spread. He was so excited when saw her that went directly for it. After they performed, there was a final admission from his mouth and her confirmation.

"We are fooling ourselves. This is something that we cannot overcome. It's more powerful than us; no matter how rationally we act," he said.

"Right. I cannot overcome it. Let me get divorced from Armand. But no matter what, I cannot wait for the divorce court," she said.

"We can go on doing it, cautiously. I need it," he said.

"Yes; I need it, too," she agreed.

From then on, they continued their illicit relations,

===

One of those days that he was returning from sharing with Morgana, the nurse was waiting for him at his office. Barbara had waited for three hours. She had asked the secretary for him and was informed that had to visit Armand Assante for follow-up. When he came back, Barbara saw him stepping out of Morgana's car. When he approached her, he had a mild smile. He felt like reporting his whereabouts but Barbara was curt and explosive.

"Don't tell me that you were doing a doctor's work. By your looks, you were doing a lover's work. Remember that I am a nurse. I can recognize a relaxed and satisfied aura. And you are freshly showered. You were fucking Morgana. You dumped me because you felt that you could 'not be good to satisfy a woman' yet you satisfy Morgana, the tigress. ¡Doing that is a feat!" she got up and left abruptly with long strides. Mormon went to his office.

Rebecca had overheard this conversation, closed the dating book, and filed the records. Then went into the office.

"Doctor Kelly, won't you give me some of your attention? I heard that you took care of the nurse that was waiting for you and she said that you were going out with Morgana. I want a piece of the action, too. Won't you give me some? Come to me, please." She unbuttoned her blouse and lowered her bra exposing her breasts. "Can you kiss me now? Here." Pointing her breasts and then spreading her legs. "You can see that I am hot and wet. Come into me, please. I don't mind if you keep going with Morgana and Barbara. Come. I want all of you in me."

"Becca, why are you doing this? All our relation is professional. It has to be," Mormon said.

"I have been waiting for you to propose. I had almost every day come into the office without underwear to make you notice what you can have, but you never do or say anything. I have been waiting for you to propose with my pussy steaming hot expecting your meat, but you don't pay attention to me, yet spend your time and spill your milk with those two."

"Becca, all we can have is a professional relation," he said. He was surprised by her crude expressions.

But Rebeca extended her arms inviting him.

"I am sorry." He walked out of the office. She started crying with an uncontrolled sobbing. He decided to get out and not come back for the day. He would be back in the morning.

===

The next morning Rebeca walked and presented her resignation. Mormon was adamant about rejecting her resignation.

"But I have to resign. I have given myself to you and you have rejected me. I have been humiliated. I cannot stand it anymore that you take other women and don't even consider taking me. I am ashamed," said Rebeca.

"Becca, please. I'll increase your salary 50%. Stay. Let's forget all that happened, I want you to stay." Mormon said.

"I am leaving anyway. You don't need to worry about your secret life with Morgana. It will always be a secret. I am sorry to leave like this. But I cannot cope with my feelings for you."

"OK. I will not insist anymore. It is now a problem of conflicts with your dignity. I am sorry for all. I cannot go into an affair with you. I love and respect you as a person," he said. "If you need a letter of recommendation, let me know. I will pass your professional availability to other medical offices to assist you in getting a new job. I wish you the best." She cried and abandoned the office. A few minutes later, Morgana called.

"How are you, doctor Kelly?" She always called with an impersonal salute which turned more familiar when he demonstrated with his reply that all was safe to talk freely. "I have news to share with you."

"I am OK. Can you share the news today during the night?" he asked.

"Yes," she said and hung up.

With some anxiety he waited to reach to the early evening hours, wanting to see her. When she arrived, he had already booked a room at a near hotel. He sent a text with the number to her cellular and she went as a visitor. When she was in his room, they showered and had dinner, and went to bed to make love. It was an interminable chorus of moans and grunts of the many pleasures that they felt with repeats and yearnings for more. When they had a break from the lovemaking sessions, she was ready to share the news and went directly into the matter.

"This morning I was waiting for Armand for breakfast to ask for a divorce. Well... it turns out that he was to ask me the same. It will be soon that we can be together and freely enjoy ourselves."

"Those are very good news. How are you going to manage that, so that he does not suspect what's going on between us?" he asked.

"Leave that to me," she said. She kept to herself the condition that he wanted to impose to divorce her: He wanted her to allow him to hide in a secret room and be a peeping tom watching them while making love. Within, she felt embarrassed, but she decided to probe the idea with some questions to him. "Doctor Kelly, I feel curious and have to make you a couple of questions. What do you think is love? How do you relate sex to love? Remember that I heard you at the party talking philosophically on various subjects. It was very interesting to me. I guess it should be interesting to hear you on sex and love."

"We can get a reference with the Babylonians; they used to have sex in public. They would lay on the sidewalk and people would pass by their side while they made love. They went on not caring for audiences. Shocking. Don't you think? I think that sex is a very private matter. When this is done by lovers it is called 'making love.' Doing that is when they relate they make love a reality expressed with the intimacies of sex. Sex is exclusive. Our handicap is that our nature prompts man to have sex once there is an erection and there is a pussy to relieve it."

"That is crude; there is no poetry in that," she said.

"That is a reality, no more," Mormon said.

"I am ready for more love, my dear. Are you?"

"I am ready, too. Let's do it," he said. And they made more love. This time at a slow pace make it last and go through each phase with the highest satisfaction. Sweat mixed with the lingering sexual smells. Then they rested, got dressed, and returned to their homes.

===

When Morgana parked her car at her home, she saw a man talking to Armand. She walked directly to them. With a slight overhearing, she could infer that they were talking about past adventures of youth. After Armand introduced her to the man, Simone was his name, he teased him.

"Morgana, his parents were expecting a girl. That's why they baptized him with that feminine name, Simone." With this statement, Morgana could conclude that they had an old friendship of confidence. "I believe that you would like to be alone to enjoy your inside jokes. See you later, Simone. I invite you to stay overnight. I can tell Manolo to ready a room for you." Raising her sight when noticed a figure pushing a cart toward them. "Here he comes. Aha, he's bringing a bottle of wine in an ice bucket. I guess I'll have a cup and leave. You are to talk a lot with some more wine. Bye. Glad to have met you, Simone."

She got to her room to clean herself, again. *This Simone is a very interesting man. I hope that Armand is not making a Cupid match of me and him. If he does not remember my condition of no interventions from him, I will remind him. He is not to choose for me. I have Mormon in mind.* Then she went to sleep. *After all, there are no sex sessions with Armand.*

Meanwhile, Simone and Armand enjoyed the recollections of their wild youth. Simon realized that Armand could not do more of their wild-youth deeds in his wheelchair. Armand decided to be an open book.

"I don't anymore have the rock-hard phallus that promises ladies frictions on the G-zone," said Armand. "A surgical intervention tickled on zones of erection and the powerful gun became a flaccid gel. So far there is no hope."

"I am sorry that you have a useless cannon. I remember that we used to chase girls together," said Simone looking at the heavens, "it is getting dark. I have to go."

"Why, Simone? You can stay. My wife made the invitation and I endorse it," said Armand.

"My business is very demanding on attention to security. We even watch during nights with these," showing a pair of night-seeing glasses. "I have to go back to my people. I never told them where I was going to be. Sorry. I have to go."

"Your business? What kind of business do you have? Tell me. Can I invest in it?"

"I am the only investor. I make sure earnings only come to my pocket. But the most important thing is confidentiality and discretion."

"Confidentiality? What do you mean?"

"See, I work on community services related to inappropriate citizens. I help the communities by getting rid of these people. That is all you can know of. Sorry. Good evening, Armand."

"Simone, can I keep the ultraviolet glasses? I have good use for them. I know that those glasses let you see in the dark," said Armand.

"No problem," handing the glasses to Armand. Then Simone left with long strides

===

Mormon and Morgana continued enjoying their lovemaking. They did some pleasing tricks that pleased each so deeply that bonded with a powerful sex dependency that they could not overcome. She captivated him when she laced her legs on his back, undulated her body, and pushed herself upward. His pleasure was so intense that he almost fainted. Wanting to reciprocate, on another occasion, he undulated his body slowly with soft motions and went deep. This kept her in a state of constant pleasure that kept her suspended in a continuous orgasm. She was paralyzed and her abundance got the bed very wet. Loving so well they were most pleased with life that they were to marry soon. Armand had consented to the husband, but still, he insisted on being a peeping tom secretly watching the couple having sex. Morgana was reluctant to yield to that and worked some evasions to prevent such invasion into their private lives.

After marrying, the newlyweds spent some nights in local hotels to secure privacy. But Armand was determined to make the watch and demanded that she comply.

"Either you comply or I make my case spreading the rumor that Dr. Kelly produced in me a dysfunctional erection with his surgery to get to my wife. When an investigation develops, I will corrupt it by paying the investigators to make it a real case. He will go to jail and I'll accuse you of confabulating with him. You will be a golden piece of gossip for our insipid society and he will be ousted from the medical associations. You will live in solitude and his reputation and professional achievements will amount to nothing." Armand never suspected that his invented threat was true.

She manipulated her lovemaking sessions to be off hours to prevent Armand from watching them. She thought that she was being successful in doing this. One day she got a surprise at breakfast. It was the day in which she had decided to decline Mormon's invitation when they had gone to bed wanting to give him a wake-up surprise at three AM. Mormon was still sleeping. She turned on some perfumed candles. Going over his naked body, she kissed him all over and paid some homage with oral services. When he was ready for her, she sat on his maleness and started a slow rhythmic motion. His motions were slow to lengthen his pleasure. She was raptured. Still in the morning, the recalling of the experience kept her in a distancing reverie. Mormon joined her at breakfast and she did not notice him. But Armand raised the volume of his voice and brought her back to the living reality.

"I can testify that these glasses allowed me to keep watch on my property this early morning. I don't need to see perfectly clearly. Just enough to identify what is going on. It is perfect," said Armand boisterous. He kept on bragging about his success. She opened her eyes and looked at the glasses and to Armand.

Morgana's cup slipped from her hand and she was dizzy, about to fall. Mormon caught her midway and prevented her from falling on the floor.

"What's wrong, dear? Do you feel OK? Would you rather stay and not go to the office?" asked Mormon.

"I am OK," said Morgana. "It's just that the special glasses on Armand reminded me of when my brother was in the military. His death was too tragic and I had not overcome it. I am sorry. I'll go to work. I am OK." She left worried. She did not even say a word to Mormon.

===

On her way to the office, she recalled that she had seen the same glasses on the second visit of Simone Rockwell. He mentioned that he had to use them the night before on an assignment of community services. Morgana wondered what services could be that required those glasses. She asked Armand. Recalling the conversation, he explained Simone's job in vague terms.

"*Simone helps society by putting out of commission some characters that hurt society. Sometimes he contracts to take care of other characters who are unpleasant to the powerful. His contracts demand great discretion. Those contracts yield him good revenues. He is rich. Very. Powerful and influential. That's all you need to know about his profession.*"

"*Oh. OK. He is a dangerous man, then,*" Morgana said.

"*For his targets, he is. Otherwise, he is low-key,*" Armand said.

Recalling this conversation prompted her to an idea and decided to see the man, alone. Mormon could be no witness to her thinking. Not this thinking.

From her ex-husband, she had learned that Simone was at Hotel D'Guerre. She went there for a business meeting. In there, she asked for Simone's room phone and called him.

"Hello."

"Hello, Rockwell. This is Morgana. I need to meet you for a community service. When can we meet?"

"Are you in the lobby or at home?"

"Lobby."

"I am readying to go down. Will take me less than five minutes. Can you wait?"

"If it's that quick, I'll wait."

Rockwell met her in the lobby. "What kind of community service do you need?"

"What do you mean 'what kind'?"

"Didn't Armand explain to you? I arrange to get rid of unpleasant people in the community." Ideas started zooming into Morgana's brain.

"Do you pledge to do it then have no way back and swear to confidentiality?" asked Morgana.

"I do."

"I want to get rid of Armand. We'll talk later for more details and my reasons for the request. I'll meet you again this afternoon to talk fees and results wanted. I want this done quickly."

===

As soon as Morgana finished her business meetings in mid-afternoon, she drove to the D'Guerre hotel. Simone Rockwell was waiting for her as agreed in her previous call. She asked the concierge for a private conference room. He asked one of his men to clear the room with electronic gadgets to make sure nobody would be eavesdropping. She was surprised at the precautions that he took.

She understood that he was in a dangerous business. His precautions pleased her.

"Well, Morgana, it's your turn. Tell me what you want to be done. Normally I would not ask 'Why' but in this case, being related to Armand, I have to ask."

"Rockwell, telling you this is very embarrassing for me but I will tell you all anyway, in spite of the shame." And she told Simone about the conditions to divorce Armand, how happy she was with Mormon, how satisfied she was with his sexual prowess and performance, and her admiration for the way he thought of love in sex. Rockwell lowered his sight and blushed moving his head sideways with his lips pinched in a line. *Armand deserves wrath or a bullet. Both, really.*

"I agree with the service that you are asking for. But let's come to a definition of the situation. All you really want is that he does not see you in your intimacies. There are various alternatives to that: kill him, blind him, relocate him, imprison him, or convince him to stop acting like a peeping Tom. Which one would you like to do? I can talk to him."

"Talk to him to convince him to relocate. If that doesn't work, then kill him. I don't want the problem to arise again in my life. I don't want anybody to invade my intimacy; I want to be free when I am with my husband. He is very sensitive to our privacy when making love and I will not confess the divorce condition imposed by Armand. I am sharing with you that I liked Mormon and was with him before divorcing because Armand's lack of erection got me desperate. I intended to divorce him but he proposed it before I did. His divorce condition is so aberrant--"

"Enough. I understand you. Don't say more. I'll have to confess to you that I intended to make a marriage proposal to you when Armand told me that he was going to divorce you. But knowing the condition, if it had been me you had chosen and you had told me his condition, I would kill him. For your case, I will not kill him. I'll follow the 'talking and relocating' step. But I will kill him if it doesn't work as you say. The fee for this case is 125 thousand for the 'talking and relocate' and 500 thousand for killing him. Deal?"

"Deal," answered Morgana. Then she left for home and invited Mormon to have dinner out. They went to a hotel and had a lovemaking reunion to then sleep at home. She was fooling Armand's condition. Meanwhile, Rockwell had some meditation to make and decided to go to the hotel bar.

===

Rockwell went to the hotel bar. Daguerre's bar was very popular for its music and entertainment. There he met a brunette. She was well shaped with wide hips and round rear, ample and firm bosom, black silky hair that covered her breasts seductively, and with round thighs that seemed to hide a delightful promise. He felt struck by her; he felt she exuded sexual delights. She smiled.

"Hello, lady. Are you by yourself?"

"You can sit if that is what you want to propose, please. OK. Now I will not be alone."

"My name is Simone Rockwell."

"Very good. You are named like my favorite character, Simone Templar, The Saint. I hope that you too have a halo for good deeds."

"Unfortunately to say that the halo would not correspond to me. I don't go for good behavior much less good deeds," said Simone. "And your name is—"

"Barbara Donella. I am a registered nurse. I saw you talking to Mrs. Morgana Lavoisier the wife of the reputed Armand Balfour."

"She is no longer his wife. Now she is the wife of Mormon Kelly. He's a surgeon. Armand divorced her due to some strenuous circumstances," said Simone.

"I know the circumstances. He is sexually dysfunctional. That is the man who was solicited by many women of high economic status. Now he is put down by those who wanted him. Poor man. His circumstance came to be in a surgery room. Mormon Kelly was the surgeon. The very one."

"Do you know Dr. Kelly?"

"I do. I suspect that he created Armand's dysfunction to get to his wife. I don't have the facts but I am looking for evidence. But I would need power to get to the bottom of it. People act very discreetly with medical records of prominent personalities."

"You have a nice piece of gossip but don't have the evidence for it. But why are you interested in proving this?"

"Revenge. Mormon led me to think that we could have a relationship and in a short time he dumped me to be with Morgana."

"I see. Is the resentment so strong that you want to make a man lose all his hopes, love, career, and reputation? Is your pride so valuable to you?" He was feeling concerned for Morgana and wanted to do good for her. *I need to discourage Donella. How can I do it? She cannot be allowed to take revenge now when Morgana is feeling happy.* With the few times he met her, he had come to gain sincere affection for her. After Morgana confessed her problem, he felt paternally protective.

"You make me feel embarrassed about my intentions."

"Glad I do. In my experience hate and revenge never pays back and leads to many problems. I would invite you to my room for a more private conversation. Would you be interested in joining me? This is early noon. We may have a private dinner if you care."

They walked to the elevator. He took her by the arm. *Her flesh is soft and firm. I like to feel her. I like this woman. I want to know her more.* He almost felt like an adolescent in his first petting meeting. It was awkward for him. He was feeling something different from what he felt for Morgana. It was not the pursuit of a sexual impulse though some of it was there. He was going to be nice and courteous with Donella.

Rockwell and Barbara had dinner and spent the night making love. A strange click happened that joined them. In her mind, the feelings of hate and perverse revenge waned. Her attention was now on this man.

"Are you OK?" He asked her. "I am all good and happy with you."

"I am OK. I am very pleased. You freed me of all negative feelings."

Good. Love is springing in her. "Would you like to be with me tomorrow?"

"By all means. I am contented. I didn't expect you to invite me for a second time."

And so went the week. Barbara did not mention her revenge against Mormon, again. This made Rockwell get more interested in her. He became a giver to her; jewels, nice dresses, and coats. He felt great.

"Are you rich?"

"No. I'm fortunate for knowing you." He would not say that to a woman unless he was sincere about it. He felt surprised by his reactions. *This is all providential now that I am considering getting out of the "community services" business. Barbara will make closure to my life and help me be happy. I feel pleased to be with her. Morgana's will be the last service I do. I will not even charge her. We all deserve to be happy when the opportunity comes. Nobody is entitled to put conditions on our happiness. I'll go to see Armand tomorrow early in the morning.*

===

The results of Simone's intervention showed in the news some months afterward. The prime news in the newspapers was the retirement of Mr. Armand Balfour.

He had gone to the country suburbs to retire. He split his business with Mr. Simone Rockwell. Mr. Simone would manage the various businesses of Mr. Balfour to keep them producing income for both. Mr. Balfour would stay out of the business activities. He will stay out of public contact for medical reasons. His residence will become the property of his ex-wife, Morgana Lavoisier, who will reside with her new husband, the prestigious neurosurgeon Dr. Mormon Kelly. Mr. Simone Rockwell will reside in the suburban property of Mrs. Morgana Kelly which she gave him in gratitude for special favors of community services. He will live in Morgana's residence with his wife Barbara Donella who is doing community service helping the poor and needy. The fortune of the new social elite Rockwell is estimated at two billion dollars and growing. He and his wife are most welcome as the new members of our distinguished society. As for the fortunes of Messrs. Kelly they sum over four billion. Mr. Balfour's fortune has gone down with the splitting but it is still a substantial one billion. It seems that the rich stick together. Interestingly Mr. Balfour retired from our social elite but has a strange contract with Hugh Hefner, owner of the famous Playboy business. Twice or thrice per week, Mr. Hefner comes with the Playboy girls along with some playmates to visit Mr Balfour, who hosts them.

The Colombian Girl
By Pedro J. Ramírez

"Joshua, I need to talk with you. Has to be face-to-face. This has to be done ASAP." Deborah had a desperate tone. "Can you meet me at Toby's café? I'll be there in half an hour. I know you are with Carla, your Colombian girl. Please, don't show up with her."

"What if I do?"

"Remember that we are still married. If I make enough noise about your relationship with her, your future will not shine. The financial world is very sensitive and doesn't appreciate people who are blatantly unfair. I don't want to hurt your life. You are a smart man. You know what is best for you. Avoid going into a black hole."

"OK. I'll come alone."

Deborah was fatally in love with him. She could not understand his rejection. She received passes and compliments from other men, admiring her sexy looks and her refinement. Her clothes had finesse and all fitted her well-shaped body. She was torn between the conflicting challenge of telling him to go to hell or submitting to him and waiting for him to straighten his feelings. She decided to call Joshua to assess what would be their relationship.

Deborah retouched her make-up, gave a few passes to her long black hair, stretched her dress on the hips to avoid her rear being too noticed, picked up her purse, went downstairs to her car, and drove toward Williamsburg Bridge. It should be no more than 30 minutes and 10 to wait for him; he was always late.

===

Joshua sped up to be on time. He wanted to appease the resentments that he had prompted in her. He went into the Williamsburg Bridge and he noticed in his GPS that the Kent Avenue landed directly into Toby's. He knew the place. He had taken some ladies in there. The place was not that fashionable but was discreetly located and the cuisine was very good. On his way there, he got distracted by his GPS and did not notice the construction signs ahead: "Bridge on Repairs" and "Detour Right." By the time he noticed the detour, he could not react on time at 90 MPH and went into the repairs stretch for a free fall of 300 feet. When the vehicle landed, sparks and gas reacted and the car exploded.

===

Deborah sipped wine and waited. He was not showing up on time, as usual. Thirty minutes have passed. This was too much waiting, even from him. She was hesitant to call him to avoid giving the impression of a fastidious insistence. After twenty minutes overdue, she reached for her cellular and called his mobile. No answer. Some news was coming on Toby's TV that interrupted the current program. It was about an accident. She decided to wait longer and turned to watch the news to kill waiting time. It got her attention that the car involved was a golden Lexus. Joshua's latest buy was a Lexus. The TV photographer scanned the scene and showed some pieces of the car spread all over. The main frame and the motor were fixed as assembled. The news would not say the identity of the driver. The unanswered phone and his not showing made a lump in her throat. A decision had to be taken and she did. But she held an apprehensive uneasiness about what she was going to do. She went to the place of the accident driven by curiosity—it was an undesired curiosity. When she got there, the body of the driver was on the stretch and the paramedics rolled it into the ambulance, still uncovered. The body was charred and could not be recognized. But she had an ominous feeling. She could have cleared her doubts by calling the Colombian girl but she was reluctant to do so. *It was funny how pride can get in the way of the right thing to do.* But her phone rang. It was the Colombian girl. Unexpected and undesired as it was, she welcomed the call.

"Was it Joshua in the accident on Kent Avenue?" Deborah was surprised. It was the first time that she heard the woman. She didn't expect this girl to speak English at all; much less with such good diction. Distracted in her thoughts, Deborah took too long to answer. "Do you hear me, Mrs. McNicky? Was it Joshua in the accident on Kent Avenue?"

"I am hearing you OK, Miss Carla. Nobody knows. They are conducting an immediate investigation." She was going to keep the lines of respect and formality to stay distant. She did not want this relationship.

"Is the car a Lexus, golden?" The ominous feelings of Deborah re-emerged with a powerful thrust, almost making her faint. Her stomach crunched. She had seen a golden fender of the car which was torn off and did not suffer the burning of the explosion.

"Yes; it is golden and I see the emblem of a Lexus." Her voice was trembling and raspy. Her throat had dried and she had some symptoms of suffocation. No more talking; had to recover. She decided to go into her car and take a sip of water from her bottle in the cooler. When she recovered, she heard the cries of the Colombian girl.

"Hush. Hush. Calm down. They don't know for sure yet who the driver is. I told you that they have to check the—"

"But, Mrs. McNicky, if Joshua is not with you, this driver of the accident has to be him."

"Your logic is right," said Deborah afraid of the logic which pointed to a true reality.

"Please, allow me to go there and see." *This was a strange request. The woman could come anytime she wanted. The accident was a public event. Why would she ask her permission?*

"I cannot forbid you to do as you wish. I am leaving now."

"Don't go, please. Let's meet. Now there are no reasons for resentments or rivalries. Besides, we both lost the man we loved. He really wanted to come back to you and I was going to lose him anyway. It will take me 10 minutes to be there." *She had it planned to go there for a meeting. That's why she was almost halfway. Why?*

So, they met. Though composed, Deborah's feelings were on the surface. It was obvious that Carla's presence disturbed her. Being a woman of high values, she expected and wished that time would heal those feelings. After all, she had to agree that they had in common the death of the man they loved.

The next day the results of the investigation were in the news. The license plate was found within the area of the explosion and they could identify that the driver was Joshua. After three more days, some strange details about the car accident stood out. When the body went through forensics they checked the organs still without burning for drugs and alcohol. They found that these had a strange drug very seldom found among regular addicts. Only found among addicts coming from Colombia.

===

As time passed, Deborah's resentments and ill feelings toward the "Colombian girl" receded and the two women started progressively sharing more after meeting at the accident scene. Carla was well cultivated and read and had a fine sense of humor. Her flow of ideas was that of a sharp mind, always witty in her responses while conversing. She was a good company to have by your side. Her appearance was impressive. She was brunette, long, raven-black hair, a delicate body but not fragile, and of good shape with round hips and a nicely curved rear. Her personality was a touch that she adorned with an outfit of good taste and matching colors.

Carla moved to the same building where Deborah lived. While there, Carla approached Deborah to make friends. In time, people considered them good friends. But Deborah had some sensitive qualms in the back of her mind: The drugs found in Joshua's body at the time of the accident were extracts of passionflower mixed with hops, kava, and balm. It was good that one of the detectives investigating the accident was a friend of Joshua and hers. He gave access to the analyst. The analyst explained that these herbs in small proportions reduce anxiety. But the appropriate amounts, if increased progressively, could induce a depressive state and lack of willpower. A person under these effects and some dosages of verbal criticizing and lack of rest would lose willpower. *The lack of rest could be easily handled by Carla with her sexual demands.* The person would be easily maneuvered by a smart person aware of the mental state produced by the herbs. All this made Deborah suspicious that she could be trying something on her as already tried on him.

Feeling that Deborah could open up her friendship, Carla decided to invite Deborah to her apartment. Carla reasoned that Deborah was emotionally vulnerable and could be reached by her intimate feelings. When Deborah was to walk in, Gloria, Carla's housemaid, showed up. Carla introduced Gloria to her. She readied a cup of tea for herself but didn't invite Deborah. But Deborah, with her usual self-confidence, invited herself.

Gloria brought the tea to Deborah and withdrew from her housekeeping chores. "Carla, do you have some cookies for the tea? Our tea ceremony here in New York reminds me of my aunt Giselle in England"

"Yes, I do. Gloria is busy now, so let me get them for you." When Carla went to the kitchen, she improvised taking a sample of the tea in her pills tube. Quickly sealed it and hid it in her bosom. After the tea, Deborah was ready to leave.

"Carla, I have to rush out. I have an appointment with some investors at my office within 45 minutes. I have five minutes to retouch and go. By the way, if you are not using Gloria's services full time, I could share her. The lady that used to do my housekeeping chores moved with her daughter to take care of the grandsons. Thank you for the tea. It was delicious. I'll come for its recipe. I want to have some more of it. Bye."

"I can concoct it for you anytime you wish. It's a family recipe with herbs from Colombia, but I can share it with you next time we meet. Bye. We can talk about you having Gloria's services on your next visit. Have a good day." Deborah rushed to her apartment on the floor below. She had many questions in her mind: She wondered how Carla could afford the apartment and the furniture and the decorations she had. All the furniture was Luxxu. There were lamps and chandeliers made of brushed brass with a Prisma center lamp, sideboards, Littus mirror on all walls, and skin-soft upholstery. People with a high income have less than what she has. Besides, she had a BMW X-3. A car like that would cost around 190 thousand dollars. She had to have a secret source of income.

After all this thinking, Deborah left for the office, where she picked up the phone and dialed.

"Is this Almuy's Investigators? Yes? Oh, ok. Mr. Gotti is in charge. I would like to make an appointment with him."

"He's available this afternoon after four o'clock."

"OK. I can be there at 4:15. Is that OK?"

"OK."

Deborah went on with her work, organizing investment notes and projects. Soon she felt dispassionate with her work. There was no joy in doing the investment analysis which she had so much fun with. Minutes later she received a phone call from Biolab, where she had submitted the sample of Carla's tea on her way to the office.

"Deborah McNicky? Would you give me your birth date and the surname of your mother? This is to make sure that you are the right person. We cannot give results over the phone unless we validate to whom. Sorry if I embarrass you with the questions. And this is all recorded."

"Oh. It's OK. I'll answer you all you need," and she went into all the required details.

"All is cleared. Now the results: The sample that you submitted could make you chronically lethargic. You should stop drinking this concoction. You will be less alert and if the dosage is increased, this could reduce your stamina and your intellectual prowess. You will live in chemical hypnosis. Your willpower will fade and you will become suicidal if you face conflicts. Take good care with this substance. I would advise you to drink something else to sleep."

"Thank you for your call and your advice. I'll discontinue it." *The bitch is really a case. Poor Joshua.*

She got ready to see Mr. Gotti, the investigator. In confidence, she explained the situation and the requests for investigation. Gotti was to investigate Carla's source of income, and whatever relationship or activity out of the ordinary. He should review his findings with her within two months.

During the time of the investigation, Deborah showed to have high trust in Carla and would frequently go to her apartment to sip a cup of tea and chat about fashions and ladies' petty matters. She was surprised to learn that Carla could easily associate irrelevant economic moves with consequences of long effects. Increased advertising of makeup, lipstick, shadow, and perfumes meant that women would be spending more on their looks, would want to lose weight, and buy more low-calorie food—but less regular food for their families. While on this, she found that Carla had a good knowledge of financial systems and online investing formats. She handled the computer with good skill. When sipping the tea, Deborah would be ready to make the effort to take a sample of it in a small plastic tube. She could do it only twice after the first time. As for the effect of the tea on her, she argued that she would take it with her medicine drops. The medicine was a chemical neutralizer that turned the tea into an inoffensive drink.

The time for the investigation review was due and Mr. Gotti was ready.

"Miss McNicky, this lady, Carla Montes, is quite a character. Her income is mostly from interests earned from her investments in various projects of high capital financed with bonds, notes, and a few stocks. We are talking about $897 million." Making a pause to let the idea sink in. "The peculiar thing is that none of the financial papers are hers. She acts as the administrator and that is why all the money flows through her designated accounts in various banks overseas. To all effects, it is as if the widower were alive. She has kept his role in his computer. For the investors, your husband is alive." Deborah widened her eyes. "She sets the holding banks where the money is to flow. "

"Very good, Mr. Gotti. Thank you. If you have incurred additional expenses, I will reimburse you."

"Oh... but there's more to share. And this additional report is what makes the lady very peculiar." Gotti's expression was of curiosity. "During the past two months, she visited a strange place in the suburbs, very inappropriate for her status. In these places, she bought herbs. Among the herbs were flowers of passion fruit. This was quite strange to me. But considering that she is from Colombia, this may be something of their folklore."

"Thank you very much, Mr. Gotti. This is a very good review. Interesting. I'll need you to go deeper into your services. I will need you to get the names of the accounts, which corporations and projects the money is flowing from-to, and how much. Can you get this ready within no more than two months?" Deborah decided to ignore the "folklore" curiosity of Gotti.

She continued to pretend to be friends with Carla, displaying trust in her. There were no noticeable signs that she suspected her activities with Gotti. Deborah never mentioned anything about Joshua's investor accounts and his relations with an investing firm. When Carla once asked about Joshua's endeavors, she acknowledged that he worked on some financial projects but that he never gave her details for which she could not volunteer information about his activities.

"He worked on financial projects of high investments but I am not related to these. When we cut off our relations, I lost track of what he was doing or the outcomes of his investments." Deborah paused and waited for an expressed relation since she noticed the crunching of Carla. "All I know is that he felt successful with the results. I would not inquire more because he was particularly discreet with the subject. You may know more since by then he had already left me. No hard feelings."

Deborah's statement was offensive and incriminating. Carla decided to charge back. "He was certainly very discreet. He was all the time, like you say, 'Hush, hush.' Well, you say 'No hard feelings' to evade the emotional conflicts that I being his lover created in you. But I suspect that you know more than what you pretend with your innocent friendship. Don't you?"

Deborah decided to be more incisive: "My dear Carla, I think that it is you who plays the innocent girl when you surpass Mata Harri probing his financial projects and secrets. Going to bed with a man still proves to be a great strategy to get intelligent details of his life and secrets. I suspect that you have many secrets and are holding them to your advantage. Am I wrong?"

"If you are implying that I had my affair with Joshua as an advantage, you don't know my feelings. You are offending me in my deepest feelings. You have not really been a friend. You are the one who works on the feelings of others to take advantage. You are a vulture. I think I hate you."

"Hate me? You have no right to hate me. It was my husband the one you went to bed with. I am the one who has the right to hate. Well, I do. You seem to have the illusion that your tea would make me forget that you stole my husband."

"I didn't steal him. He came to me on his own because you were a failure in bed. Do you realize that?"

"Oh, yeah! And you are a licking good chicken. What number did he make in your list?"

"Get out of my home, witch."

"I'll finish my tea first."

"Aghh… you, you."

Deborah sipped her tea and left, almost looking upward.

It was time for Gotti's review. The findings were phenomenal. When Deborah compared the list of the corporations and projects that his widower managed with what Gotti had researched, they were the same. Both went out to see their lawyers and certified the documents of the cash flowing into Carla's accounts from the investors' accounts. If something happened to Deborah, the evidence would take care of Carla in court. The local judge was apprised of the case and Gotti had copies of all evidence.

All seemed so easy considering that Carla was a serious case of deceit, but still, Deborah was a little undecided though did not have any knowledge to suspect that something could go wrong at court. But she was concerned that Carla always acted emotionally impermeable. She wanted to make sure that Carla paid for her faults, no matter the cost.

Deborah went to see Carla, evidence in hand, with two officers and Mr. Gotti. Then they went to the judge at the court. The judge sentenced Carla to home imprisonment and under custody till the case will be re-examined in court for a final decision. She turned to Deborah.

"Sad thing for you to see that the evidence will turn against you. Do you think that I believed in your fake friendship? I tried to get rid of you but you got an antidote to get over my beverage. The leftovers in the cup that you sipped gave you away. You are not the only one that thinks of using a laboratory," Carla said while distant from the Judge. Then turned to the Judge.

"Honorable Judge, I have a few things to say. Can I have your permission," said Carla.

"You have my permission. A constitutional right."

"This lady, Deborah McNicky, is accusing me of the things that she did. All those acts that she is charging me with were all done by her. She appropriated investments from the accounts of her husband, the late Joshua. He was my lover, I admit that. But for this, I know his fears of what he expected her to do. What he feared she did when he died. He told me several times in our intimacy that she probably had plans of killing him to do a major fraud. The killing happened when she dated him to talk; he died in an apparent accident. I can conclude that she estimated the time when he was approaching a road construction close to the Williamsburg Bridge. Then she sent a signal to his cellular. This distracted him and could not see the prevention signs. Going at around 100 miles per hour, he could not stop on time and went into the void. He crashed down from the bridge at 300 feet. Then she got control of the investments. Since then she has been getting the benefits. As of now, these benefits amount to 927 million dollars. You can send them to check her computer at her home. But not only that, Honorable: She worked on the system to make a signal with my name to incriminate me and accuse me like she is doing today. You can send for this to be investigated by somebody with knowledge of computer systems. But, beware; she has to remain here to prevent her from tampering with the evidence."

"Bitch, how could you–?" Deborah said.

"You think that you could fool me making friends and pretending forgiveness to get into my home and even drinking my special tea?"

Deborah jumped on Carla. She was close enough for Carla to whisper in her ear. "Now you will learn what my Hydra computer system can do to the identities in your computer program and what my personal cloud can do with your data. You fool; you walked into my trap by taking me as the ignorant 'Colombian girl.' And you made the double fool in hiring Gloria for your housekeeping. She assisted me greatly to get into your computer. She is not a housemaid; she is a contracted computer specialist. You have been educated to be a good person. I was educated by the street to take advantage of others. Pity on you."

"Arrest Miss Deborah McNicky," the Judge said. "Get Mr. Camtrell, the computer expert, in court and take him to Miss McNicky's apartment to check the evidence described by Miss Montes."

Camtrell went to Deborah's home and confirmed Carla's accusations. The Judge released Carla and kept Deborah in jail. Deborah was away for some time.

===

Deborah was reported at her job as being "Out for an undetermined time." Carla checked at her job for some months and they reported her the same, "Out for an undetermined time." She has not come back to her apartment, either. By now she is rotten in jail, she concluded.

Carla decided, however, to be careful and wait longer. One year has gone by. Carla called the court asking for the status of Deborah.

"Hello. I am calling to learn about my niece Deborah McNicky. I understand that she had been accused of fraud and need to know how she is and when she'll come out to see if she needs some help. I want to visit her. My name is Carol McNicky."

"Well, Miss, you don't have to come over since no code forbids informing that your relative McNicky passed away. She turned nuts and hung herself with the mattress cover. I am sorry for this news," said the mayor.

"Oh, my God. When did this happen?"

"Last week." *It was a good precaution to wait a little longer*, thought Carla. *Great. Now I can go to pick up my money. Now INTERPOL will not be after me for fraud.*

In four days Carla went for all the accumulated money into her account in Latvia. Her bank was conveniently close to the International Airport of Riga, by the Gulf of Riga in the Baltic Sea. The distance of Latvia from the USA and Colombia made it safe. If necessary, she could move and live in Russia.

===

At the bank, she complied with the formalities to withdraw her money. "How much money you want to withdraw, Miss Montes?," said the banker by the Baltic Sea.

"All of it, please." Suppressing all her emotions of victory and pressing her lips to avoid a smile.

When her bags were filled, she took care of them and motioned her two bodyguards to go in front. Three men surrounded her and four more flanked the bodyguards. A lady dressed in black, shielding her face with a Pamela, approached her in front and lifted her head. Carla recognized her with disbelief. The three men nodded to her.

"You! I was told that you were dead."

"You have your charade and I have mine. Money can buy lots of services from good people. Camtrell explained how computer Hydra changes all. But they leave a track that can be followed when coming back to the point of origin. Then their immediate final destination can be retrieved. The final destination of your Hydra was this Latvia bank. The judge, in turn, advised that you had to be caught with your hands on the money and have witnesses. You have your hands on the money and here are the witnesses. These three gentlemen, with their business formal looks, are leaders in the Russian mafia. They own over 70% of the investments that you have in your bag. Thus, they understand that you are stealing from them. The judge does not have jurisdiction in Latvia. Don't expect him to protect you from these gentlemen. The circumstances dictate your destiny. Bye, smart Colombian girl."

The Knot
By Pedro J. Ramírez

The green of the pastures was bright and shiny. The flowers were blooming with delightful smells. Some were torn by the breeze. Some petals floated perfuming the air. Rosaly's skin felt taut with the cold air. Her spirit of sixteen to seventeen was joyful with the scenery, the mild intoxication of the misty air announcing a later rain, and the message of orchids perfume lingering in the air. At brief moments the damp odors of the surrounding lake interrupted the smells, like a slap getting you back into reality. Rosaly ignored these brief interruptions and started getting ready to go into the lake. Unbuttoning her clothes, her breasts showed, then lowered her skirt and rolled down her panties and the rest showed. She was naked with gooseneck pimples on her body and a soft brilliance on her skin hair. But her beauty was not only shared with nature. Somebody was watching her at a high temperature and with feelings of great delight when seeing her soft curves with shapes that were a promise of pleasure. His powerful erection made the call to get closer and see better and more of those soft curves. He approached with the steps of a cat, cautious not to scare the innocent bird. He watched her swimming and waited. She didn't notice him. When she came out to get dressed, he covered her face and made a knot to the cover on her neck, pulled her into the bushes, and laid her softly on the grass.

"What are you going to do to me? Let me go. Who are you? Let me go. Let me go." He didn't answer.

He caressed and kissed her breasts, spread her wide, and she felt a piece of warm meat going into her intimacy which was sticky wet. She felt some pain and some pleasure. He was not rude; he was gentle. She stayed silent and curious about her feelings. Shortly after, she heard a grunt and felt something spilling inside her. She felt the thick liquid with pleasure. It was much and warm. This made her muscles tense and she lost control of herself wrapped in strange and intense sensations. Pain and pleasure mixed inside her. She let her go and could not keep a long moan to herself. He stayed inside her for some minutes, breathing hard, holding her tight, always silent, and then he pulled himself. He left her silently. She undid the knot and hurried to get dressed without bothering to cleanse herself. She didn't feel unclean or stained by his dense spill. Some of it flowed out between her thighs. *Why do I have these feelings? Was I desiring this to happen and was making myself vulnerable by going to swim in the lake in the woods? What has happened in my body that made my muscles like steel cords and then soft like flaccid rubber? Why I could not hold the long moan? Who could be this man? What held him from being rude or cruel? He behaved caring and lovingly. Had I been chosen?*

In the past Rosaly's adventurous spirit got her in trouble. But all those that happened she could solve. She was a child. This one was different. Now she was about to be a woman. Realizing that she was raped made her worry about getting pregnant. This is what she heard could happen to a girl. But she did nothing to prevent it. She could have gone back to the water and cleaned her insides as the elder ladies used to comment. She allowed it. She was in voluntary exposure and quiet submission. It was as if she had aligned to a superior plan. Was it destiny? When she got back home, she decided to tell her mother what happened.

"Ma, I need to talk to you.

"Aha. Say it."

"I went to the lake in the woods for a swim and was raped. Never saw who did it. The man didn't even speak. He covered my face and head with a dark and thick piece of cloth and tied it to my neck. I resisted at first but I felt his arms so strong that I was afraid that he could kill me. But he was gentle and caring. Never rude or brutal. He seemed to care so much that I could say that he was loving. Could it be that he was in love with me, Mom?" She decided to skip narrating the moment of intense pleasure, her moaning with delight and not feeling unclean when he left.

In the middle of her shock, Rosaly's mother considered the girl's observation. This kept the mother from the scandal consideration and redirected her thinking. "Strange as it could be, I think that he *is* in love with you."

"How could this be possible?"

"Men have strange ways, my dear. Now, don't let your father learn about this. Let me talk to him," she said with serious concern shown on her face.

But Aliana delayed telling her husband that his little flower had been deflowered. Days went on and she felt embarrassed.

By the twenty-fifth day, Rosaly expected signs of her regular menstruation. No signs. She let some more days pass. It didn't come. This much she knew about the pregnancy. She decided to buy a kit for pregnancy tests of the ones that she saw at the local drugstore. But she bought it from a drugstore in a city a few miles away from home. The test turned positive.

She relayed the news to her mother. She anticipated a scandal in her mind. Her father was too straitlaced about these matters. But he had to be told. Anyway her belly would tell him. That was, for sure, the wrong way to tell him.

"Doruk, I need to talk about a very serious matter with you."

"Not now. I'm just arriving from work. I have not even washed myself to eat and you want to add new burdens on me. We'll talk later. OK?"

"I said it is a very serious matter. Didn't you hear me?"

"OK. What is a serious matter for you?"

"It's about Rosaly. She's pregnant.

"What are you saying?"

"Now you understand it is a serious matter, right?"

"How the hell could that happen? She doesn't even have a boyfriend? Had she been hiding something?"

"She was raped when swimming at the lake by the woods. The man covered her face blindfolding her. She doesn't know who is. All she knows is that he was gentle."

"Now, now. Is she in love with the unknown rapist? Was she skinny diving and alone?"

"Yes. She was both. It is as if the man was waiting for the right opportunity. He seems not to be a pervert. I think that he is in love with her and for some reason did not approach her."

"Damn. Damn. Damn. You have been watching 'Criminal Minds' too much. This is all I needed. My daughter is pregnant without a husband, you profiling, and us living in this small town of sadness and gossip. It's ironic it is called Holyoke," he said, strung and with tight knuckles, "Where is she? Rosaly, come here, will you?"

Rosaly walked in with unsure steps and stayed distant. She was pale, tears in her eyes but her figure held elegance and poise. The father looked at her body to see a signal of pregnancy—there was none.

"How do you know you are pregnant? I don't see a sign in your body."

"I made a test with a kit I bought. It came positive. I went to a drugstore a few miles from here to avoid the people of this town."

"You did good. I don't want anybody around here to know about this. Would you go for an abortion? You should not have that creature. It was conceived out of marriage."

"Father… I will not abort. Please let me go somewhere else. I'll go to live with Aunt Mildred in New Jersey. There I will deliver and stay there. Never come back. You'll not have a reason for shame."

"Why did you go for a swim at the lake, naked? Are you an exhibitionist or were you looking for this to happen? Don't answer. Just get rid of the baby. I don't want to see him… or her. We will not talk more about this," he walked out with his right above his head making a fist, "she doesn't know the man who fucked her. What a case!"

Rosaly started sobbing and shaking. She felt dismissed from arguing. Humiliated. Her mother came to her.

"Hush, my dear. I believe you. We'll solve this problem. Do you, really, want to keep your baby?"

"Yes, mother. I am against abortion. It's a crime to the defenseless. I don't understand how Father, being so straight, asks me to do that."

"Don't worry. You'll go to Aunt Mildred in New Jersey for some days. From there you should go somewhere else to avoid your father. I am not to argue with him; it is a waste of time and gets everybody upset."

"Are you for serious?"

"Never more serious. I'll visit you there. Go and sleep for a while. When everything is ready, I'll wake you."

Rosaly went to her room and Aliana went to the phone and dialed her sister-in-law.

"Mildred, good day to you. Yes, yes; we are well. Hear me now. I need you to listen carefully. Don't have much time. We have a little predicament and I need you to be very understanding and help us, me and Rosaly." Aliana explained all the details of the raping—she would not call it so—she decided to call it 'an imposing sexual relation'—and the problems that had with her brother.

"Do you believe her all she told you?" asked Aunt Mildred.

"I do. You know that she had always been a girl of truth in her mouth and doings."

"You are right. I believe you and her. This brother of mine is a case of moralities. Good that he never met my husband. You know." Mildred consented to receive Rosaly and her pregnancy.

===

Rosaly's father was told that the girl would go to stay with Aunt Mildred to deliver. He did not oppose. His expression was of relief. Three days after, Rosaly was with her aunt in Salisbury, Delaware. She had moved from New Jersey two weeks ago when she retired. Doruk did not have her new home address. It was something that she would not share with her up-nosed-morality-brother. The aunt was a third-time widow; a detail which she never revealed to her brother. She didn't allow her brother to meet any of her husbands and kept him ignorant of her lifestyle.

The night of Rosaly's arrival, the aunt held a meeting with the girl in the kitchen. The aunt took some cold cuts from the refrigerator, and both sat to converse. It had a translucent roof held in place with a square of aged wooden beams. The stars were visible in the clear sky. Close to the colonial gas stove was a round table of mahogany coated with soft brown layers of lacquer. It was covered with a cloth down to half the legs and on it two placemats. Both with colorful flowers of pastel colors. A crystal bowl of encapsulated white roses was in the center of the table. The steam heater maintained the right temperature in the room. The place was cozy. All in the environment prompted conversing about family matters. The aunt was part of the scene in a way: She looked peaceful. In her face were not the traces of the family scandal that Doruk portrayed. She had long hair. It was pepper gray as if showing that she had experience and was ready for more seasoning from life. Her shapes were mature but attractive for a woman of nearly fifty. She was a woman who took good care of herself. Her skin was smooth and taut and her face did not show wrinkles.

"How did all this calamity come over you, dear? It is a pity, really. Your mother already told me. But there is one thing that I need to clarify with you. How did you figure that the man was so affable and loving with you?" asked Aunt Mildred, while chewing a slice of Georgia-cured ham with a chunk of cheese.

"It is not something to reason because it's not the expected attitude in a rapist by what I hear. But he had gentle manners with me. I can testify that he was caring as if not wanting to hurt me. I feel embarrassed to say it, but he caressed my breasts and kissed them with delicacy, and at the moment of... hum... eh... penetrating he did it slowly to avoid hurting me. Making short pauses. He was so loving that I gained an inner feeling to yield. Aunt, Oh... I feel so embarrassed. I felt a very strong sensation of pleasure. All my muscles started getting tense, he noticed it and kept doing it to me. I thought that I would faint. When he noticed that I relaxed, he stayed inside for some minutes and pulled his thing. And, Oh Jesus. This is most to my shame: I wanted him to go on. I don't understand this mix of feelings. When he got away I didn't feel anger. I have to admit that I enjoyed it when he grunted and spilled something warm and thick inside me. I was not mad at him. I wanted more of him. It was like a primitive sensation. But he left after my moaning. I don't know him. And to complicate things more, I am pregnant. You had three husbands. You have experience. Can you explain to me all that happened? I need to understand."

"Of course, you need to understand, dear. I will tell you from my experience." The aunt then proceeded to explain to her all the details of what had happened. It was a short course on the mysteries of lovemaking and the crude carnalities of sex. In the end, the aunt added her conclusion.

"This man loves you but I think that he is afraid of some consequences for either him or you or both. Perverts never have an attitude of love toward their victims. They just want to rape and that's it; they are concerned only about their satisfaction. This one kept on until you enjoyed your 'relaxation', as you say. You had an orgasm—the climax of pleasure in the sex relation. That doesn't happen when there is no love. He cared for you. But this is an incredible situation. Shut your mind to it and go on with life. Now is the time to rest. Go to sleep. Have some food. You have not taken a bite from these cold cuts. Eat something; an empty stomach makes poor thinking. Then we'll talk more about my husband. Mostly of the third one. He was a fabulous man."

"OK, aunt. I may skip the food. It is late to eat. I need to sleep. I'm tired. I'll be ready to learn from you when I rest. I want to have my mind clear for all that is to come."

"OK. We'll do as you say. I insist that you should take a quick bite to pacify your stomach."

"OK, aunt. I'll do that. Just one bite. I'd prefer Gouda cheese." She took her bite and went to the room that Mildred had arranged for her. Mildred went to sleep, too. Rosaly felt relieved after revealing to her aunt the pleasure details that she skipped when talking with her mother and slept well.

===

At home, at Holyoke, Rosaly's father, Doruk Sliver, tried to investigate who was the man in the lake that raped Rosaly. He made his investigation very discreetly, only asking for an unknown man in the last weeks. He could not get the results he expected. People in the surroundings were reluctant to cooperate with him because he had always treated them with social distance and with an attitude of moral superiority. One of the neighbors, Herman, a man of the same moral attitudes, mentioned to him that a stranger, a young man, had been in the vicinities of the lake about two to six weeks ago.

"But I don't have the name of the young man. All I can remember is that the girls around here were very interested in him for his looks. But he was not from around here. I don't know where he came from. He looked like a fine man of good manners. He had brown hair which he combed perfectly, not a single hair astray. White complexion. Nice features. Had the looks of an Englishman. He spent a few weeks in the surroundings. Most of the time he was around the lake. Never spoke unless a question was addressed to him. His answers were short."

"Where did he live? Did he have a cabin?"

"No. He was with two more. They raised tents of the ones that have all the conveniences. They drove an SUV and a car to carry all. When they finished their time, they left. No goodbyes. Just left early in the morning. They dressed well. The two looked like bodyguards. Didn't look like gangsters. Fine men, too. They seemed to serve the young man because he ordered them things to do. Is there anything wrong with the young man?"

That must be the man who raped my Rosaly. But, how do I find him? She would not share much information about him. She seems to protect the man. Could it be that she knows the man and is protecting him? No; it doesn't make sense: she would not come to tell me that was raped.

"Thank you, Herman. No; there's nothing wrong with the young man. I just felt curious about him because the girls mentioned him and didn't see him around. That's all."

"How's Rosaly? Makes some time that I don't see her. Say my regards to your wife. Have a good day, Doruk.

"They are well. Yeah. Bye."

I could involve more people to investigate. I am afraid that they may ask questions that I don't want to answer. Maybe I should quit investigating considering that Rosaly is at some thousand miles away with her pampering aunt, my sister Mildred. I will not go through any shame. I don't have the age for that. I'll drop this.

===

Mildred got up early, brewed coffee, baked six cinnamon rolls, and got Rosaly out of bed. They had breakfast. Mildred ate three of the cinnamon rolls and scrambled eggs. The young woman had only the rolls. Rosaly was anxious to solve some mysteries in her mind.

"Aunt, you referred to the third husband as a 'fabulous man.' Why was that?" asked Rosaly with her seventeen curiosity.

Mildred was ready to tell her intimate stories. The aunt explained with graphic details her lived excitations and pleasures to illustrate why the third husband, Richard, was fabulous. The niece was surprised and opened her understanding to a new dimension of man-woman relations. When her aunt was about finished, Rosaly gave a new conclusion.

"Then I can say that my unknown man was fabulous, too. He seemed to be very concerned about my satisfaction and he was tender before and after doing it," and stopped to think for a while, "and I can understand that he had to have chosen me to be so caring. But, how did he choose?"

"You are right on this idea. I don't have a clear idea how he could choose. Did you participate in a beauty contest, a drama, a show on TV; anything that may expose you to the public?"

"The only showing of myself had been on Facebook. But I do so with proper clothing. Oooh, wait! I remember that somebody posted some pictures of a group that was on an excursion at the lake by Highland Falls. In that picture, I displayed fully and was standing in front. I was in a black and white bathing suit. That was a few months ago. Let me look for the portable to show it to you," She went upstairs to her room and came back. On her way, she turned the PC on to be ready and show the picture to her.

"My God. You look like a living prescription for the sexual desires of a man. You look so sexy and attractive. You are in there like a blooming flower, ripe and ready for pollination. Do you understand what I mean?"

"Now that you explained to me about men, I do. But there is no way I could identify who the man who raped me could be."

"I am sure that you will find the solution to this riddle. Or God will bring the solution to you. I pray so. Let's drop it for the time. Don't anguish yourself more. Relax. All will be solved. I'll pray to God to solve it. Let's go out for some shopping. We need to buy groceries and new clothes for you. If so happens, I will introduce you to some people in town and some neighbors. Get ready to go out at one O'clock."

Rosaly was pleased with the idea to go into town. The aunt offered to buy all she needed. She would be prudent and choose only basic items for a young woman. Mildred took her to a fanciful and expensive boutique to let her select the clothing she liked.

"Make the choice you may wish and don't worry about the cost. I'll take care of it for you. And get used to places like this," volunteered Mildred with a smile. "I have the money for this, don't worry."

"This is very expensive. I am afraid to even look at the garments."

"I told you that I have the money."

"How come you have this much money? All I heard from my mother about you was that you worked in the City Hall offices. I felt embarrassed to come to stay with you and be an economic burden."

"I didn't tell you all about my husbands. My first husband was a drug lord. I didn't know it when I married him. But I found and kept it to myself. He was very wealthy and opened an account in a safe under my name. The records would say that the money was mine before marrying him, so the government could not confiscate it if he was processed for his unlawfulness. He was killed by another drug lord. After mourning him, another drug lord courted me for some years and offered to marry me. He admired that I didn't snitch on my first husband. He was very gentle. I accepted marrying him. After all, I knew this world and got used to it. He was good but died of cancer and provided more money. A third drug lord started courting me. He was very loving and romantic. This one made me fall in love with him. And he was an excellent performer in lovemaking, I will never forget him. He died three years ago. He had a heart attack. He was not obese but he was under constant tension for the business and his heart could not stand it. He was always very worried about me. All these husbands have made me some relations in that world by marital considerations. That helps me to live alone and be safe. The unlawful know that I am protected by these lords. We are very safe at my home."

"This is all awesome. Does mother know about your husbands? Did she meet them? Did father?" asked Rosaly.

"She met each one. But she would never talk about that to keep me from problems with your father. My dear brother is too straight up and moralistic. That's why you never heard these stories. Yes; she met them and she didn't disapprove of my relations. She got along fine with each one of them. They favored her. I never introduced them to your father. With his straight morality, I would have problems and he could be disfavored. Or even killed."

Rosaly had more questions to make to her aunt and her aunt was very liberal in answering them. With this mutual disposition, their family bonds grew stronger. Rosaly felt at home with her aunt. She decided never to go back to her hometown. This fostered in them a mother-daughter relationship. Her mother came two or three times per year to visit them. The father stayed distant; would only phone her when her mother came, with the excuse of learning about his wife. Her father did not want to face the shame of his daughter's pregnancy and did not want to live the reality of an unwanted grandchild. In due time, Rosaly gave birth to a boy.

===

Seven years went by. The kid grew up with the protection of the aunt and grew strong and smart. The presence of Aunt Mildred in her life made people around her refrain from making questions about her father or her status. She was simply accepted.

During those years she met various mafia chieftains who proposed to her but she declined and each respected her decision in deference to Aunt Mildred. The son of one of the mafia chieftains, who expressed not to follow the ways of his father, courted her. But despite the decency of Edgar, she had her concerns that he may later reject her son as part of the "package" in the relationship. She was worried and kept searching who could be the unknown rapist with whom she enjoyed sex in her rape experience by the lake.

One of the chieftains, who was a close friend of Mildred's third husband, stayed close to them and became like a granny for the kid. He was the one in charge of casinos and betting schemes. He did not want to work with the great money makers, like drugs and prostitution. These other business setups he saw as war camps. He was happily married and a fair husband. For this he was welcome to Mildred's home and shared the relations, pampering the kid.

"Say, Rosaly, what you may need, and I will provide. If the boy has a need say it, and I will take care. I have made a trust fund of one hundred thousand for his future studies. Every man should study. I don't have grandsons and I want to. But my son is studying in England and France and he will stay long in there. I hope he doesn't become interested in studying in Germany and perpetuate his stay in Europe. He seems to be evading something in his life. I want Ivan to get married and stop studying and give me grandsons. I want to see them. I'm already old enough." Dinoso confessed this to Rosaly and Mildred with a mix of joy and nostalgia. Others witnessing. "My son is coming back from Europe in six months. He is there under the custody of two loyal bodyguards. You'll meet him."

During her relationship with Edgard, his emotional attachment intensified and he started talking about marrying. Rosaly was not sure about taking this step. She wanted her son to be loved by a father. She postponed the proposal of Edgard. He could not resist anymore. He wanted to have the woman. Rosaly didn't want the man. But she was after social approval. Her aunt had a different mental setup.

"Rosaly, my dear, you have been too much under the influence of your father. Don't follow that. He has the greatest capacity to make a woman unhappy by dragging her into his moralities toward unhappiness for the sake of social approval. Don't accept to marry looking for approval. Wait."

===

By the time little Zeke was to be eight years, Ivan returned from Europe. While unpacking at Dinoso's home, he put aside a picture in a thin frame of gold covered with grooved glass. It was a picture of a group on an expedition and swimming in the river. The room maid noticed the picture and picked it up to place it on top of the chest. He hollered to her.

"What are you going to do? Don't touch that picture. It's for me to see only. Nobody else has to do with it. Now get out of the room." She left quickly.

By this time Dinoso proposed to celebrate the return of his son and make it a joint birthday celebration of Zeke and his. The birthday of each was apart for two days. Mildred made good contributions to celebrate the part of her nephew. She really referred to him as her grandson since she did not expect to have any—she sent her children away to live with other relatives so that the affairs of her husbands would not hurt them. With this, they distanced for so long that their sentimental attachments to her waned completely. They only wrote once in a while. Only when needing money. With their practice, she decided not to answer their communications.

This was going to be Ivan's party but he did not want to go to it.

"My son, how could you refuse to go to this party? You'll meet lots of good people. If you don't go to it, you are bringing me shame after I proclaimed this a good day for me. Besides it is my birthday celebration. You'll meet my adopted grandson, Zeke. I expected you to have given me a grandson. But you have not, so I adopted one. The most gracious and smart kid that you may meet." And the party was and Ivan went to it.

There was a good mix of people at the party. It had reps from various countries. Each brings exuberant gifts and plenty of money.

"You, all be generous when giving to Zeke. He's starting to live," said Dinoso sipping wine and inviting the guests.

Ivan stayed in a corner away from the cluster of people. His bodyguards made a shield around him. People could hardly get close to him. One of the bodyguards separated to pee. When he was going into the restroom, he made a cautionary glance toward his back when he saw a lady that he knew. He became pale and nervous. When he went to the urinal, he had a hard time running the zipper of his pants and urinating. When Dimitro came out of the restroom, his pants were wet on the pubis and the crotch. Another of the bodyguards started laughing but Ivan silenced him with a look. Dimitro leaned and whispered to the ear of Nari.

"Remember the lady that struck the boss when we went to that little town? It had a ridiculous name related to tying an ox and something religious?" asked Dimitro.

"Stupid. The city is Holyoke. I remember it," said Nari, "Since then… well he has not recovered from the guilt and from the fear of being rejected if he confesses raping her. He had spent years traveling and studying and he had not been able to put her out of his mind. He does not admit it, but at night he has dreams about her. But he is afraid of facing her. He had thought of going to the place but he would not; ashamed of what he did. He does not know her name; only her looks."

"Well… if my recollection is not wrong, that lady is here, in this party. I did not investigate anything about her to avoid being a suspect. I can swear that this is the same lady, now a woman. I heard things. The child on this birthday is hers, he is called Zeke. Edgard, the son of the Moroccan chieftain is proposing to her and wants to marry her. He is hot for the woman and wants to marry soon."

"We cannot let her marry Edgard," said Nari. His tone was a little too high and Ivan threw a dart for a look.

"Nari, what is wrong?" asked Ivan, looking at him and then at Dimitro.

"Nothing, Sir." They had so many years together that the answer came out in unison.

Nari went to Ivan with a petition.

"Sir, would you let me go to get some food? I am starving. Will take me a couple of minutes." Ivan granted. Nari took off and mixed with the people. All were happy, drinking, eating, and talking with laughter. On the walls and tables, they hung balloons that floated its many colors.

Soon he was close to Rosaly and took a careful look at her face. *Yes; this woman is her. I don't know how things like this could happen but I see that it is happening. If this were planned, would not happen so perfectly. I will need to talk to Edgard. He is not a friend and I don't know how he may react, but this woman has to marry Ivan instead of him.* He started looking for Edgard. Finally found him talking with Dinoso by the table of wine and cheese cuts.

"Sir, can I have a word with you?" addressing Edgard but looking at Dinoso for consent.

"What do you want? Aren't you one of the bodyguards of Ivan?" questioned Edgard with the tone of somebody of a higher category. "Don't you see that I am talking with Don Dinoso?"

"I noticed, Sir. But this is very important."

"I expect it is because I am making serious plans with Don Dinoso. Say what you have to say."

"I don't think that you want me to say it right here, Sir. It is something about you. It is very private."

"And what could that be?" replied Edgard. "Say it now."

"I insist we go private if Don Dinoso excuses us."

"Don't make me lose my patience. Say it now."

"It's your choice then," said Nari. "This is a little embarrassing."

Nari narrated the whole incident between Rosaly and Ivan. How it happened, his guilt feelings, how he had yearned to be with her, his shame, his fear of rejection though wanting to go to Holyoke to look for her, confess, and marry. Edgard didn't feel very grateful for this news and his reaction was quick. After hearing the first sentences, Dinoso made a sign to one of his men to bring Ivan.

"I am not going to give up this woman. You have created that story to open the opportunity for your boss. She's to be mine," said Edgard. Ivan was walking in.

"Nari, what are you doing here? Go back to your place. There are more bodyguards in here with my father," said Ivan.

"He is not going to go, not now," interrupted Dinoso. "I want him right here explaining what he just told Edgard. And you are to tell me if he is saying this shameful thing that you did at Holyoke is true. Talk again, Nari."

Ivan heard with profound attention. He was amazed. In a burst of anger, he punched Nari making him bleed from his nose. Nari was stunned with a mean look to Ivan but repressing and not threatening.

"But, boss, all I do is help you to reunite with her so you don't suffer anymore. I have heard your yearning and dreaming with her; you crying in the night as if you had a nightmare. You should join her. Don't miss this opportunity."

"You fool. Won't you count what she thinks or feels? What if she hates me for what I did? I raped her!" Ivan lowered his face, ashamed. He knew what his father thought about situations like this.

"How did you make up your mind to do that to this young woman? At that time her age was seventeen. You had twenty-one. This is a technical violation even if she consented to it. That means jail," said Dinoso. "I hope she does not accuse you."

With the commotion, Rosaly and Aunt Mildred came to where Dinoso was.

"What happened? What's wrong?" asked Mildred. Ivan looked at Rosaly. His look was intense and Rosally was trying to understand why. It was the first time that she saw him. Something from him was familiar to her but she could not define it. She went to him but he turned his back to her brusquely and left the place. Nari and the other bodyguards went after him.

"What's happening, aunt… what do I have to understand? Explain me," said Rosaly

"I have to understand first to explain it to you, my dear. Let's go back to the party. More music, please. Serve more wine." The musicians started a new piece and soon everybody put the event behind them. Everybody but Mildred. She had heard the words "technical violation." She made it a point to ask Dinoso what had happened. Or Nari. It was Nari who told her.

===

Edgard, determined to have Rosaly, driven by his strong desire for her, went the next morning to see the lawyer of his father.

"Can you check out for me if at Holyoke in Nebraska raping a seventeen girl means jail for a man of twenty-one?"

"I don't need to check it. This is a Federal statute. This is so at any State."

"Can I make an accusation from here at Salisbury?"

"If you have the right evidence."

"I do. The admission of having done it and witnesses" said Edgard. "Here's the name of the man, the witnesses of the confession, and the witnesses of the act. All you will need to do is call them into court." The lawyer read the name and the description of the act.

"What? I advise you not to do this. Even your father will be against it."

"I want to do this, regardless. You do it or I'll get another lawyer. But I will tell my father that you had been overcharging your fees. Make a quick decision and contact the police station to get him arrested TODAY."

"Shit! I don't need this kind of situation. OK. I'll do it. What do I tell your father?"

"Say that I am very much in love and determined to have this woman."

The accusation proceeded and, during the afternoon, Ivan was arrested and taken to jail. Within a week, he was to be processed in court. The prosecutor called the witnesses and all testified confirming the rape. Nari and Dimitro wanted to improvise a lie but Dinoso forced them to say the truth. They had no choice but to abide or risk their lives. Edgard was all for himself and with the spirit of a hot wolf determined to have Rosaly. Ivan was hanging in there; waiting for the outcome of the events. His guilt made him a secluded soul, jailed in the perceptions of himself. Caged within his mind. His only frame of reference was the rape he committed and how punishable this was by disgracing the life of a young woman and disrupting her family relations. He wanted to get condemned to be free from his guilt. His father waited patiently and shared his feelings with Mildred and his wife.

In the court process, Rosaly learned about Ivan and his self-entrapment. She was emotionally paralyzed. She could not be questioned. Edgard had been managing her emotions. Her dependency on Edgard was obvious and morbid and he exploited it to satisfy his desire for her. Her shame for the feelings of the rape made her silent. Edgard perceived that he could enslave her with all the consequences and lead her to accuse Ivan as the rapist. But to do this conflicted with the sexual satisfaction that she felt during the rape. She still recalled Ivan's gentleness and soft caressing. In her mind, she had wished more of him. She admitted that she fell in love with the unknown rapist. She hated her condition of being a woman raped—it was dishonoring—but she wanted to know the rapist and have more of him. Feeling ashamed of her conflict of emotions, she was afraid to talk in court.

Saying her real feelings would be morally disapproved. Whatever she said would shame her aunt who had been good to her. Herself didn't matter anymore. The summary of it all: raped, pregnant, protected by her aunt, delivery, and continue living. "Protected by her aunt" was the event to respond to with gratefulness. The rest of the events were inevitable. She could go on living with Edgard. She burst into tears in the middle of the process at the court. The Judge asked her to step down and she went to her aunt.

"Aunt, I cannot talk. The witnesses confirmed all; I don't need to talk. I can go on with my life the way it was to be before the rapist… was known. Don't you think? Please help me."

"The help that you need is more within you and has to come out. I cannot help you. You have to help yourself. Tell me what's in your mind; what's in your heart. Don't hide anything from me. Open your heart. What do you really want to do?"

"Oh, aunt, I feel so ashamed. I will tell you anyway. When I came to you I was open enough to let you into my heart, but now… all these people around us. I don't think I can talk," said Rosaly. And she told the conflict that she had in her soul that was tearing her heart.

"Just be honest with the court in front of Ivan. His father had condemned him for what he did to you. If you are open when you talk, you'll free him, and yourself. After you were raped, you untied a knot but you did not untie yourself. Now you can untie the knot within you that will let you be free and meet the rapist face to face. Now you can demand from him and he will give you what you want. Edgard will not be able to give you the love that you want. Only Ivan can. Choose to be free and free him. He loves you and you have been expectant to find him because you love him, too. Your decision, hon." Rosaly swallowed and stood facing the Judge, nervous with a trembling voice. She had decided to talk.

"Sir; I need to talk. This time I will open my heart to the court, regardless of how the court may judge me. What I will say will be morally disapproved. But I will say it anyway. I know it will help. Ivan's repentance and feelings of guilt shown in his crying at night and his embarrassed shyness to come back to talk to me reveals his heart. He felt aggravated, and repented, by what he did. And rejects himself but I don't reject him though I reject what he did for how it has affected my life. Considering, however, how my life now has changed, I see that it was God's design to help me. Who can oppose God?" Rosaly continued with the details of the rape and the consequences she lived.

The narration went on for over an hour. Edgard was with his jaw fallen and his mouth open to a drip. His neck veins pulsed and welled with madness and his face reddened with intense fury. He had been ridiculed. The feeling was so powerful that he went for his Glock and aimed at Ivan, who was sitting by his father, Dinoso. Bang! Close to that very instant Ivan leaned back to hear Dinoso who had shifted to talk to him. The bullet past him for a fraction of an inch and got his father on the head who was sitting in the same line of the bullet after Dinoso. His father was a dead man. The court security approached Edgard, guns ready. At Dinoso's signal two men behind Edgard put back their guns into their holsters. He realized that he could have been killed at that instant by Dinoso's men. Immediately he was arrested and confined for prosecution. (Prosecution was better; the other lords would handle the situation with terminal gravity.) With the commotion, the Judge cleared the court. A few minutes after, he called Rosaly and Ivan into his office.

"Young lady, by what you did, you are a woman of great courage. Don't feel shame for feeling for a man. This is what makes a real woman," then addressing Ivan, "Learn to appreciate this young woman who has confessed her love and her wants for you. In the future, I don't want to hear that you hurt her. Keep on being the 'gentle rapist' and love her. You are sentenced to one year of community service thanks to her testimony. Don't forget that you could have been jailed even with her testimony. But I am to do justice and that does not go by the letter of the law. Have a good day. Marry her."

Dinoso and Mildred got up and each went to the respective kin and put them face to face.

"Time for love and no more regrets, repentance, or embitterment," said Mildred.

"Yeah. Son, hug and hold her and promise to marry her and make a happy life. I'll go for my grandson."

Gay Obsession
By Pedro J. Ramírez

I had finished reading Hamlet. I have as many conflicts as the poor prince. He wanted to be with Ofelia but she felt committed to keeping within the rigors of her society. The force that kept from being with the prince, the Latins call it *pudor* and is associated with shame and distancing. The Americans call it *modesty*. But this is related to humbleness. I capture that the Latin meaning implies more the feeling that imprisons me to be shy with the man that I love so much. For his love, I had done so many disturbing things. Stealing, lying, accusing, and making false representations. And many more things that risk my high status in society. Pudor prompts a discreet feeling of being rejected. Modesty marks the bearer with a special touch to produce a personal distinction. Why should I be feeling *pudor*? It is because of Grace. The precious jewel that my man is in love with. If she were not there, I would not suffer *pudor*. How can he come and say that he loves me yet feels free to walk around with her holding hands and kissing her in public? I live frustrated. I want him to live frustrated, too. Or make her live frustrated. That is the way it has to be: the same for each. I have to be an equalizer of affections. I will be the "love equalizer." I have to work out a plan. I must do it with intelligence, not lose the love of my man. I love him too much to lose him. I have been tolerating his affair with Grace because she is very gentle with me. She does not know that I am his woman. I show myself masculine enough to presume to be virile. But no more. She is separating him from me. This has to stop. He knows that he is my man. I was in his life before her. I will study her and her life to get to her vulnerable habits. I envy her pussy. Here comes my man. Now I have to squelch my thinking and feelings.

"How are you, Abdón? I have been wanting to see you. Will you be going to my apartment tonight?" I asked. "I am needing you."

"I will not. Grace invited me to her apartment," said Abdón.

"Will you be making love to her? If you do, save some for me. As I said, I need you. Try to be early there so that you rest and have some time for me, too."

"Aren't you asking for too much?"

"Why is this 'asking too much'? I am before her in your life. Just for that, don't you think that I should be taken care of first?"

"Maybe you are right. But..."

"But what? What do you want to say?" I asked. "Are you wanting to say that you prefer her pussy? Now you come to me with that when for years you had me and no pussy. It was me the one who put you in the university and pays for your car, and your clothing, and gave you a place to live and food." His twitchings showed embarrassment. His nervousness made him shift from one foot to the other, and bend his head scratching the neck. I enjoyed the scene of the powerless. Abdón's macho character dissolved when I confronted him. His physical beauty made him a delightful toy, a good piece of meat that a gay would like inside. But meant nothing else. I liked him because I enjoyed him and could control him as a powerful matron. He lived in a separate apartment, which I paid so that I could presume virility.

"Would it be OK if I go to see you first, Igor?" asked Abdón.

"That is better though not completely satisfying," I said to him. "You will have to start reviewing your priorities. I would like you to stay with me when you make love to me." Abdón lowered his head, yielding. In those moments, I wished he would be a man of bigger balls. I would enjoy him more. His dependency bent his will. Manhood is important for gays, too.

Early during the night, Abdón went to see me. At my apartment, we had very satisfying sex. I enjoyed his powerful thrusts into me.

We were two exceptional bodies enjoying their skin and meat. But still, I envied Grace with her G-zone. That zone is only for vaginae. God should have provided the rectum with a G-zone. Pity me.

After he took care of me, he showered and added touches of perfume, shaved, and then went to see Grace. I decided to go and peep. He was so excellent with her. Their sexual activity stays alive in my mind. It is alive after weeks. I have not dared to peep again because the jealousy that arises in me is too abrasive inside me.

Their experiences were out of my imagination. The delights in them were beyond my conceptions. My envy crept into my heart and my liver. When I saw them, I felt my mouth with so much bitter bile taste that the sweetness of a chocolate Lindt could not overcome it. Now, I feel like a piece of walking acid. I am in a toxic mood. My hate for Grace flows inside me like a spiraling fire of blue flame. I hate her guts and envy her body shape and all her holes which have the adornment of her hips and meaty rump. I presume that she has a fleshy vulva, too. He bit and licked her in the middle to her frenzy and ecstasy. She was so elated that almost fainted. When she was demonstrative of her pleasures, he admitted being dizzy of gusto for her. How is it they can feel that much? Envy keeps creeping into me. To imagine them is torture. To recall what I saw tortures me. To figure out their other levels of pleasure is torture. Their living together tortures me. I have to end this. It is impaling my soul to a wall of hatred. But how? It grows more every day. My envy is killing me.

They cannot live together. I have to separate them. She will pull my man away from me. I have to see her, talk to her. On the sixth week, I visited her, when he had to be 150 miles away to realize a project work for his last year of university studies.

"Grace, I imagine that you love Abdón very much, don't you?" I asked her.

"I do. But why your question? What does me loving him have to do with you?" said Grace. It seems that I could not hide an expression of concern and she perceived it.

"Nothing particular. I just felt curious."

"That is a funny question just walking into here. Why would you be interested in how much I love him? That is not a question that other men ask unless it is a father."

"Don't be so obnoxious. All you need to do is answer my question."

"I don't have to answer any question related to my feelings for Abdón." Grace was now looking at me with curiosity, like wanting to explore my brain. "What kind of relations do you hold that require me to answer your question?" She was spilling the fruits of her studies as an investigator.

"Nothing particular." *I could not confess that I have been his woman for years. If I did, that could bring me new problems which could affect my income of millions. Sorry. My social prestige will be thrown back. My contacts. All will be lost. Death is better.* "My relations with him are those of a good friend. What are you thinking? I am just concerned with his wellness."

"I am only following my instinct. You are so particular in your manners. Too correct. Like a gentlewoman of society."

"Gentlewoman? What do you mean?" I asked. "Discretion is not in your traits it seems." Then I started to turn to go.

"Don't go, Igor"

"Why not? You are toxic." And left. I was afraid that she might keep pushing her questioning, irritate me and lead me into a blunder. Her studies on investigations have turned her into a chronic agent of mental probing.

===

I went to the woods to free my thinking. I was feeling stabbed by jealousy and envy. In my secret cave in the forest, I could think freely, without interruptions, and cool my feelings of jealousy and envy. It had all the comforts I needed. The forest was an expansive piece of land. The cave was deep into the forest and very hard to locate. It was at the downslope on top of a mountain, hidden by trees and a mild fog. It was in a natural depression; it could not be seen from around the mountain. Being a millionaire provides exclusivities. I got it built by foreign constructors who were instructed to be very discreet. This was a place that I only knew of and which I was careful not to reveal to anybody else. Not even Abdón, in spite of loving him so much. The only place the people knew of in the forest was my cabin. But it was seventy miles away from the cave. I have had some parties with a selected few, very rich people of great influence who had very private lives. Even to them, it was a secret that I was female to Abdón. The place was not inaccessible on foot but bears, wild hogs, and constricting snakes were around it, plus insects with dangerous bites like arachnids, centipedes, and scorpions.

In the forest, I stayed two weeks away from business and from my love. My administrators and accountants took care of all business operations. They were honest and of a clean record. Businesses did not worry me. The constant beating in my mind was Grace. Doing that peeping disgraced my thinking and my life. Envy is not good. Many evil thoughts came to my mind. It was like having a devil whispering secret plans to hurt Grace. I deposed all those plans to avoid hurting my love. Love always inspires a sense of nobility.

That sense of nobility was disrupted by Grace one night when I was looking for my love at his apartment. She was there visiting him. He ignored that I had returned from the forest. I used my key to get in. She was on top and very active. When she noticed me, pulled the blanket and covered their bodies.

"What the hell are you doing here? How come you have a key?" Looked at me and then at him, and asked him, "Are you with him? Do you do it to him?" pulling herself from Abdón. "This is incredible. I want to be the only one who gets your dick." With a realization in her mind, "Either you quit this freaking faggot or me. But you cannot have both. Sorry." Turning to me, she spat, "You get out of here now." With an attitude of indifference. "I want to finish what

I started." Then went back to top Abdón and started her motions, looking at me mockingly. "Get out. You cannot do what I can do. You need a pussy to do it."

I lowered my sight. I felt so humiliated that I had no reaction. My mind went blank. So I decided to leave without saying a word. My assassin Russian ascendancy was blocked. Abdón looked ashamed but did not react either. The pleasures were still lingering in his body and looked toward me wanting distance. When coming out the door, I heard both coming. His was a grunt and a moan. Hers was a long moan with exhaustion and some exclamations. Then I heard their wet, smacking kisses. I cracked the door to see. She remained on him, leaning her body on his chest. He caressed her butt and pinned a finger in her ass and rubbed it. They were getting ready for more. She pushed herself for deeper penetration. I could not stand it and jerked myself out to my car and left. Hot tears rolled down my cheeks, bitter tears. But in my heart, mixed with the emotional tearing, swelled an overwhelming hate for Grace. *This time I will not talk; I'll act and punish her, regardless of the pains that he will suffer. His suffering will be like a crucifixion for me, too, but I will do what I have to do. I will go back to the forest for deeper planning.*

===

Talking to myself, I did the planning to get even with horny Grace. I came to realize that going to the cave would be the best place to do my "works on her." With my plans, I had to do some changes to the place but that was not a problem for me. I could afford this with the money that I have and more to come. I built a hidden prison under the cave, a separate room for torture with tools, and a gas chamber. My fantasizing for revenge led me to create a detailed frightening weird world. This will be the fall of Grace. I'll need a man. This time I'll put conditions to my advantage. When I was ready to execute, I posed as a conciliator, a maker of peace, inviting them to my secret place.

"You are very special persons to me. I want to invite you to my most private place in the forest and make a new start in our relations."

They accepted the invitation. After two days of sharing time at my place, Grace made a confession that I did not expect.

"Igor, I am pregnant. I have three or more months," she said with a spicy look and a smile of triumph. It seems that Abdón had delivered her our secret relations. Her triumphant smile was supported by her ability to have children which no matter how I yearned for it, I could not. I felt beaten. She was perceptive to notice how I felt. Quickly added another cruel pun. "Only real women can conceive children with the seed of a man. This is a gift that only God can produce. Neither money nor technology can do it."

At her remark, I decided to go to the kitchen. "I'll prepare some entrées and then sit to converse with you. You can drink wine," pointing to the wall cabinet, "there are the bottles and the glasses." In the kitchen, I cried. I could not realize if I cried for envy or because I felt morally responsible not to take action against her because could risk her baby. I recovered when I became aware that later I could hurt her deeper by taking her baby and redeeming myself. I cooled and went to them with the entrées. We did some chit-chat and went to rest. The whore was anxious to prove her pussy-power. From my room, I could hear her moans. She had hopped on him without showering. Really horny. His final grunt was heard and then silence.

I could not sleep. By around three in the morning, I saw Abdón's silhouette at the door. He was naked, walked to my bed, and made love to me. It was for me an experience of loyalty and his lovemaking was perfect. I didn't want to lose this man. His formidable prowess left me satisfied and exhausted. I could then sleep. I cooled my hate for Grace and refrained from my vengeance to avoid hurting her pregnancy. We stayed a few more days and then left to take care of my various businesses. Grace was very pleased with me for sharing my secret cave. When we arrived at their home, held a short but meaningful conversation. Abdón went to the bathroom to take care of his needs.

"I feel that I know something more about you which you have not shared with others. I am into a secret of yours. When you are part of those private matters a deeper friendship develops," she said. It was for her to discover that this is the closeness that the Corleone mafia family fosters with their enemies to gain their confidence before terminating them.

I decided to follow her line of thought. "Yeah. This brings a pleasant sensation to feel minds and hearts joining," I said. "When is it that you will deliver the baby?"

"The doctor says that it should be by the middle of August. We'll be in the hurricane season. I hope that he is not stormy, hahaha."

"On October he'll be strong to travel and you should be healed. We could go back to the cave. It is very safe and fresh and will help you to recover from the exhaustion of the delivery that you have been through. You know, kid, husband, housekeeping." Her face glowed.

"Oh; that will be a real treat. Will you do that for us? You are very generous. I'll tell Abdón."

He was walking in to join us. "Not necessary to tell me. I heard. Definitely most generous, Igor."

"Good. It is booked then," I said. "We'll set the date at another opportunity. Abdón have a good night. I intend to have a better night. Bye, now." The statement 'I intend to have a better night' was my invitation for him to come to my place. He would sedate Grace for a deep sleep and he would sneak out to make love to me. I left to get ready for him. I wanted to be his pleasant woman. Competing against Grace was no easy feat. She was attractive and well-shaped. Her seductive body would lure any man to make love.

===

We three returned to my town office. Abdón was to visit me. I carefully shaved every hair of my body. I was careful with my skin. He felt me, he used to say, like creamy and licked and kissed me all over, caressing my butts and biting them softly, then all my back and the tip of my penis. He provoked in me all the sensations that could come out of my body. When he arrived he was ready for me with a powerful erection. He did not hesitate to grab me and turn me over for his pleasure and my delight. My expectations were to feel his deep penetrations with hard thrusts. I was a fulfilled woman in his strong arms. In no instance would I resist his masculinity or propose being the male. I never competed with his wants. My role was to please. When he left, I was drained of sexual desires. His prowess was still active. I was sure that he would take Grace, too. I woke late and went to my office. It was eleven. Abdón had already arrived. His energies were always high he looked almost glowing whereas I looked like a soul in depression. He signaled me to go into the office.

"We have to have a short conversation. Let us go private." We walked into my office. "Please roll the blinds. Nobody should see us. And lock the door. Could you also tell your secretary that you do not want to be interrupted?" I suspect that my face was a question mark with my eyes open, but I did all that he told me.

Before I could open my mouth for a question, he unbuttoned and dropped his pants. "What are you..." I was to ask, but he put his index on his lips.

"Shut up. No talking. Just come here and do what you do good," he commanded. I knelt and got his piece in my mouth licking and sucking getting it deep into my throat. He grunted and I got a gift which I swallowed with gusto. That made my morning. I recovered my energies to work. While walking out, he said, "Special service. You should feel better for the rest of the day."

Definitely my depressive mood was gone. *That is my man. Oh, God, I cannot live without him.*

===

Like that were my days of happiness with my man. Grace was the impediment to my complete satisfaction. She had to be put out of our lives. Otherwise, I would not be happy; and I deserve to be happy with my man. Once into that thinking, my mind went into my past.

I still remember clearly my adolescence. The girls in the neighborhood admired my figure, all my looks. I was like a sculpture. Girls of more experience used to say that I was a nice piece to eat. Younger ones already into the hormone flashes of attraction, looked at me with greedy eyes. I suspect that they "salivated" in their vulva. Some dared to kiss me.

All those demonstrations and comments my mother saw as signs of danger and protected me from them with some harsh comments that made a shield around me. In spite of this, the girls looked for me and wanted my company. I used to share poems and talk of movies and romantic literature with them. My father and my older brother criticized me with caustic remarks.

"You love too much to live in the world of the sissies. You should be playing football, baseball, or basketball. You spend too much time with the girls," said my father. "Come with me to fix the motor of your brother's car. Earn the right to drive it, too."

My mother would come to protect me and revert his orders, "Leave him alone. He has to do an assignment on how to raise a child. He should not be getting dirty with grease now."

My brother would top the situation: "Hahaha, he is the other young lady of the house."

My sister would embrace me and invite me to chat with her with a second invitation: "Let's go to my room and talk while you iron my dress. I'll be going out with Mark and my ironing is not as good as yours. Come." I did the ironing feeling useful to my sister who had a sensitive deference to my feelings.

These ashamed me. More and more I became distant from the other boys, who also bullied me for my sensibilities. Some boys with similar traits would make friends with me. It was great that some of them were strong, athletic, knew karate, and had more friends that were of my temper. These were very attractive young men. I had strange sensations when I had them near me and enjoyed their hugging and embraces. When we went to the beach I liked them to look at me when I undressed. One afternoon, a strong one came to me and caressed and kissed me on the mouth. It surprised me that I responded with erotic sensations which electrified my whole body. The touching and caressing went on and soon was desirous of being penetrated like it's done to a woman. He did. I felt a powerful erection and, after some more strokes and his meat thrusts into me, I had an orgasm. From then on I wanted more of this. It was easier than with girls and nobody would get complications of pregnancy and none of the silly complaints of girls. All that it required was discretion. Mother and father never learned about my fascinations. If somebody tried to expose me, I would ruin his sexual reputation. If it was necessary, I would pay to accomplish this.

I always acted very cautiously and would pair only with carefully chosen partners. As years passed, Abdón entered my life. He was so passionate when making love to me that was inevitable to fall in love. He responded with gentleness and delicacy. Soon my heart was his and could not help voicing my need for him. He never took advantage of my need and was very loyal. On my own, I provided for his studies, house and food, and generous money. Despite him being attractive to many women, he was loyal. Sometimes a raging jealousy went deep into my soul. He stayed loyal. We met weekly to make love our way. This was a most happy relation.

He was more mature when Grace showed up in his life. I considered his relations with her a good idea and promoted the idea of them having sex and getting married. This way people would see his relations with me as friends. Our relations have to stay secret. If that became public, I could lose millions in the businesses that I was managing from my inheritance.

But now Grace was pregnant and I have the impression that Abdón is in love with her. He confessed it. He never confessed love to me. My love does not pull him as her pussy. I cannot be separated from him. He has to be mine forever.

These intense feelings for him prompted me to devise a plan to be the only one in his life. My body aches for him.

===

Some years ago I had the courage to ask my man how he had gained such graces to charm a woman. I was hesitant to do so because a woman is to respect the privacy of her man. When I asked him, he was gracious to answer with candor.

His father was a great influence in his life. "It was my father the one who taught me about women. He used to say 'Women make all efforts to control a man and rule his life, and ruin it, too. Man always looks for power but yields to her pussy. Don't let a woman rule your life and your wishes with her pussy. Take her, rip her virginity, and enjoy her but be cautious when she takes a stand to control you with your desires for her pussy. When she can do that, you become an idiot and act without conscience of your benefits. She will try to get you to feel love for her. But this is all due to her wet piece. If you quit one and get another, you will feel the same love once you have her piece. The minute she is raising her pitch to control your life, discard her. Discard her permanently and get another woman. You'll be happier. And don't forget: sons or daughters are yours even if you leave the mother.' My father was really rough about these ideas. He considered men more virtuous and more loyal. 'A good man will be more loyal to you than a good woman. He does not have a pussy, so what? The important matter is to have a hole for your dick. Don't forget this, my son. Never.'"

"Do you know the reason why your father lived with such ideas?" I asked. I was shocked. I never heard somebody express such ways. Much less have his son follow the advice.

"Do not know. All I know is that my mother and two previous women that he had eloped with another man. One of the men, the one who took my mother, came back to my father. He wanted to raise me with my father and live as his woman. My father accepted. I had two fathers. This is how I learned to live with you."

"That's why you are so gentle. You learned from your father. Are you rough with women?" I asked.

"No; my father taught me to treat women as delicate creatures. But he emphasized being firm with them. He advised me 'Keep them in line. Show them that you are determined so that they don't take your words lightly. Your relationship with them should be conditioned so that they understand there is a consequence if they don't abide by your requests. Don't forget that either, my son.'"

He was a mixture of vinegar and sugar. I felt that treat on me. It only happened with words. I wanted to be the submitted woman, always pleasant and available for his pleasures. I enjoyed him very much.

===

August. The time came for her delivery. She delivered a beautiful child. Abdón was ecstatic about the baby. He kept looking at it like an unbelievable event; a miracle. He looked at the baby immersed in reverie. When somebody called him, he felt pulled out of a dream. I could not compete with his mixed loves. I took some final decisions. These were fostered by the new laws allowing marriages of the same sex with the ability to raise a family. Abdón and I could marry and the baby could be adopted and make a family. Grace had to be out of the picture so the man would be my exclusive. Another fake wife could be by his side but his love will be mine. I waited to make an appropriate execution.

Six months after the delivery, she was already active with Abdón. I would not give an opportunity for another pregnancy. That would get him out of my life and I never considered killing him for leaving me. I had to act quickly for they behaved like bunnies. I had a harder time getting him to see me once per week like we used to do. I invited them to my cave

Us three went up. For two days we shared easy conversations about petty matters, most of them related to the baby. On the third night, I signaled him to see me early in the morning. He sedated her and she went to sleep early but I knew that she would wake shortly after. I had given her a stimulant that would overcome the effects of the sedative. Half an hour after she went to sleep, he went to my room and started making love. She got up and went to my room. I knew that she would hear us. I noticed the door cracking open. I expected the worst from her madness.

Abdón was having his orgasm after me having three when suddenly she stampeded into the room and sank her nails into the back of Abdón. With the pain, he was flaccid soon and pulled out spilling his milk on my butt. I rolled over and covered myself with the quilt. She started hitting him hard.

"Bastard. Don't I give you enough sex to get a man besides me? Don't ever come to touch me, again. Why do you have such waste of milk on the ass of this stupid when you could spill that in me to get me pregnant? No matter how much you may want it, I will not give you my sex. You are dead to me. I want to go back to home now. NOW. Get ready."

He was shocked but composed and stayed cool. "Go back to bed. I want you now. To bed, NOW." He spat his vinegar of which she was afraid.

Her sight lowered and she had an incredible reaction of obedience. She went to bed and he washed, urinated, and made love to her. She did not moan, she cried loud with all kinds of erotic expressions that would flatter any man as the macho. I was baffled and understood his mix of sugar and vinegar for such an influence on her.

After her session of delights provoked by mine, she kept a sulky mood, distant at all times. He tried to persuade her for all three to live together, sharing him in peace. When he proposed the idea, she grabbed his crotch and expressed her thoughts.

"This is mine. Exclusively. I don't want to share my dick with anybody else," she said with a lustful expression shown by biting and licking her lips. "This is mine. Only mine."

I looked at her with a blank expression and turned my head and looked at him. He gained a new understanding of her and secretly made an agreement with me that I did not expect.

During the night, he sedated her again. But this time there was no stimulant to wake her shortly after. He invited me to do what I never expected. We wrapped her in the sheets and carried her to the torture room. He had explored the cave changes. There we laid her on the tool bench, then he spread her legs and went to a closet, pulled a jar with some insects, unscrew the lid, and placed its mouth on her crotch. A few insects came out and got inside her. Her body twitched. He injected her with a full syringe with a dormant.

"This will make her sleep deeper and not pay attention to the itching inside," Abdón said. Now let's go to your bed. When she wakes, the job will be done. We don't need to worry about her body."

In my room, we made love again. He took longer to reach his orgasm and I enjoyed him inside me for more time. We were a happy couple without impediments and with a babe to nurture making a family. All that was needed was a new wife to make the social facade. One that will not need to learn about my cave, unless she provoked his vinegar like Grace did.

www.ingramcontent.com/pod-product-compliance
Lightning Source LLC
LaVergne TN
LVHW091548060526
838200LV00036B/744